A Rebel Against the Cause

A Tennessee Unionist in the Collapse of the Old South

Scott Allen Freeman

Blue Dragoon—Boise, ID
Paperback ISBN: 979-8-3303-2119-3
eBook ISBN: 979-8-3303-2124-7
Title: *A Rebel Against the Cause: A Tennessee Unionist in the Collapse of the Old South*
Author: Scott Allen Freeman
Digital distribution | 2024
Paperback | 2024

This is a work of fiction. The characters, names, incidents, places, and dialogue are products of the author's imagination, and are not to be construed as real.

Published in the United States by New Book Authors Publishing

Dedication

For

The men and women of the Idaho Civil War Volunteers who have brought "living history" to the public for decades.

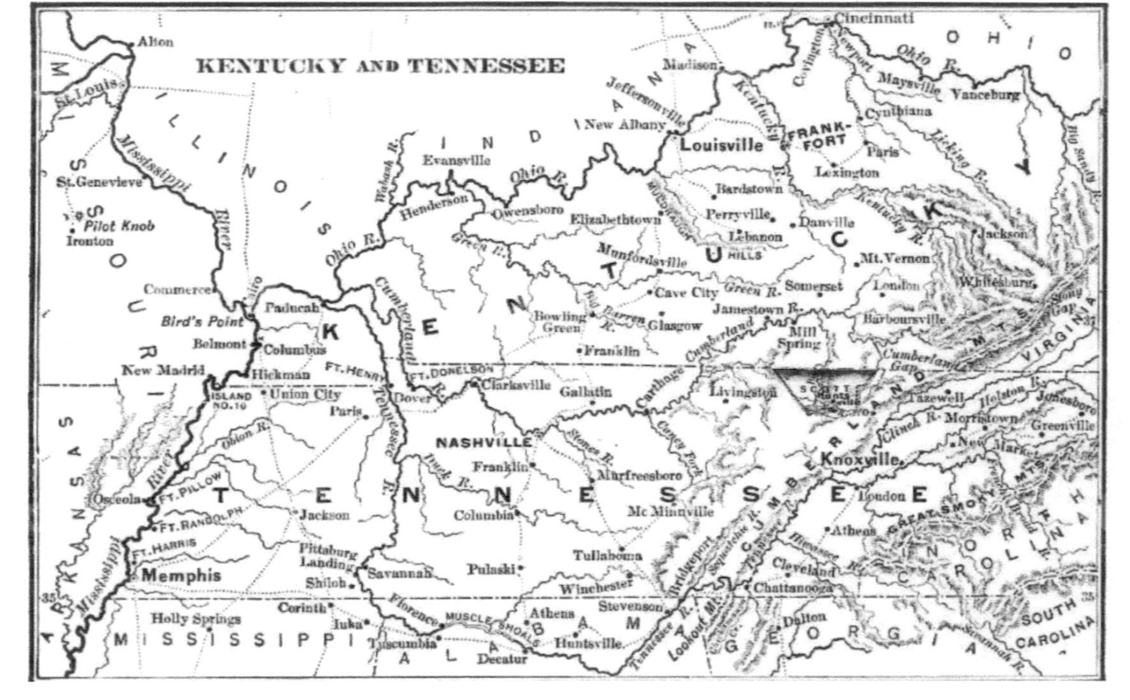

KENTUCKY AND TENNESSEE
ILLINOIS
INDIANA
OHIO
MISSOURI
ARKANSAS
MISSISSIPPI
ALABAMA
GEORGIA
SOUTH CAROLINA
NORTH CAROLINA
VIRGINIA
KENTUCKY
TENNESSEE
Mississippi River
Ohio R.
Cumberland R.
Tennessee R.
Green R.
Wabash R.
Big Sandy R.
Licking R.
Clinch R.
Holston R.
Duck R.
Stones R.
Caney Fork
Florence
CUMBERLAND MTS.
GREAT SMOKY MTS.
U HILLS
Alton
St. Louis
St. Genevieve
Pilot Knob
Ironton
Commerce
New Madrid
Bird's Point
Belmont
Columbus
Cairo
Paducah
Hickman
ISLAND NO. 10
Union City
Paris
Ft. Henry
Ft. Donelson
Dover
Clarksville
Osceola
Ft. Pillow
Ft. Randolph
Ft. Harris
Memphis
Holly Springs
Corinth
Iuka
Shiloh
Pittsburg Landing
Savannah
Jackson
Tuscumbia
Decatur
Athens
Huntsville
Stevenson
Winchester
Pulaski
Tullahoma
Columbia
Franklin
Nashville
Murfreesboro
McMinnville
Bridgeport
Sequatchie R.
Chattanooga
Cleveland
Dalton
Athens
London
Knoxville
Carthage
Gallatin
Livingston
Jamestown
Mill Spring
Franklin
Bowling Green
Glasgow
Cave City
Munfordsville
Elizabethtown
Perryville
Lebanon
Bardstown
Danville
Somerset
London
Mt. Vernon
Barboursville
Whitesburg
Cumberland Gap
Tazewell
Morristown
Greenville
Johnson
Louisville
FRANKFORT
Lexington
Paris
Cynthiana
Covington
Cincinnati
Maysville
Vanceburg
Jeffersonville
New Albany
Madison
Evansville
Henderson
Owensboro

Chapter 1
An Uninvited War

The broken, boulder-strewn terrain in Eastern Tennessee's hill country is sparsely populated, but generously supplied with caves and rocky recesses that can provide temporary refuge to a man on the run. For a young man of twenty, hiding out in the woods was safer than remaining at home in 1862. Lester McGill had been holed up for days in a natural shelter formed by a rocky outcropping that kept the rain off the eight-foot square living area he carpeted with fallen leaves and pine boughs. In this part of the Cumberland Plateau, much of the forest is dominated by tall evergreens, ideal for screening the refugee's camp from view. His campfire was fueled with fallen hardwood branches and gave off no telltale smoke. Lester was only two miles from his home near Huntsville, seat of Scott County, Tennessee and he knew he couldn't hide out much longer without being detected by Confederate soldiers or partisans. He was determined to head north into Kentucky, but he first needed to learn the position of the nearest Union soldiers, where he'd be sure to find friends.

Lester had just turned twenty during the previous month, December 1861. His early years had been peaceful and mostly uneventful; not much happened in Scott County and his neighbors preferred it that way. Those with land were primarily subsistence farmers who grew corn, raised hogs and chickens, and usually kept a milk cow and vegetable garden. The land was not suitable for raising cash crops like cotton or tobacco, so there were few slaves in the county. The northern border of Scott County follows the Kentucky State line. Knoxville is only forty miles to the southeast, in the fertile valley of the upper Tennessee River. This part of the valley was home to larger, more prosperous operations. South of there, the counties along the North Carolina line feature the imposing Great Smoky Mountains.

Most citizens of Scott County did not embrace the South's slave-based economy and culture. They resisted inclusion in the Confederacy and, like most Eastern counties, voted against the ordinance of secession that was passed in the wake of President Lincoln's call for volunteers to suppress the rebellion. Scott County cast the highest "no" ratio in the state. Though largely symbolic, the people held a vote to secede from the Confederacy and proclaimed *The Free and Independent State of Scott.* Similar independence movements were seen in Jones County, Mississippi and Winston County, Alabama. Secession was unpopular in areas unsuited to plantation agriculture, or where the citizens depended on commerce with the Northern states. Mountainous regions like the Appalachians and Ozarks, counties along the navigable rivers, and some port cities held Northern sentiments. For Lester and his people – called Unionists, Tories, loyalists, Lincolnites, anti-secessionists – refusing to serve the Confederate cause made them targets for Rebel violence. In turn, hostility toward the Confederate occupiers by armed anti-secessionists, plus the presence of lawless guerrillas, made Eastern Tennessee more deadly than the battlefield.

The Confederate army considered defending the upper Tennessee valley to be of highest strategic importance. The Memphis and Charleston Railroad was the only direct rail and telegraph connection between the Atlantic coast and the Mississippi River. Its tracks followed the valley upstream through Chattanooga and Knoxville, and then ran east into Virginia. The grain crop in the valley helped feed the Rebel armies, another reason to maintain an occupation force with headquarters in Knoxville at a time when men were needed closer to the front.

The people in East Tennessee were feeling like captives in their own homes. Earlier, in November 1861, several Unionists were executed for attempting to burn the railroad bridges across the Tennessee River in advance of Union troops that were promised but never sent. Four of the bridges were destroyed and Confederate soldiers grew more abusive. As the guerrilla conflict escalated, Tennessee men, sometimes with their families, were escaping into Kentucky, a slave state that did not secede. Both North and South fielded armies in that critical border state. It was no secret that the U.S. Army was recruiting and training infantry units at Camp Dick Robinson, established near Lexington. Enough Tennessee men had made the perilous trek into Kentucky to fill two new regiments.

Confederate troops were guarding most of the escape routes into Kentucky, especially Cumberland Gap, which cuts through a long, forbidding, sometimes vertical ridge at a point where the borders of Tennessee, Kentucky, and Virginia meet. Back in Washington, Mr. Lincoln was keenly aware of the plight and the need to relieve this loyal area, but one general after another had to acknowledge the near-impossibility of supplying an army along any route except up the valley from the West. Chattanooga would have to be taken and held first, so there was little hope for the relief of East Tennessee.

The home he leaves behind

Lester had been living in a tiny house that he rented near town since his father died in 1857 and his mother moved in with relatives in Knoxville. He hadn't met many of his mother's kin; his few relatives in Scott County were on his father's side. This was the only community Lester had ever known and it was with much anguish that he reached the conclusion he was no longer safe there. Embittered, he swore he would never support a Confederacy that made him a fugitive from his own home in a climate of violence where Rebel soldiers grumbled about fighting an *invisible enemy*.

With no land to farm, Lester had learned a variety of skills that enabled him to do odd jobs around the community. He began with only a few tools, but sometimes his client could furnish tools necessary for the job. Later he approached the blacksmith in Huntsville who agreed to teach him the farrier trade, involving shoeing and hoof-care for horses. It was a valuable skill, but with no shop of his own, he helped part-time at the smithy and then worked the rest of the time on odd jobs, sometimes for clients he cultivated at the smithy. He had an easy-going, engaging personality that earned him the goodwill of his clients and the friendship of the general neighborhood. The sight of Lester on his horse, saddlebags jangling with tools, was familiar to the people on Scott County's back roads. As time went on, he could mend harness, patch roofs, repair farm equipment, fix fence, and help in the fields at harvest time.

Often one of Lester's jobs would require the help of one or two local slaves, who considered him their friend. In the South, the skilled crafts were often performed by slaves, so Lester was able to learn new skills from working with them. As the war approached, Lester was growing more and more convinced of the immorality of slavery. Yet in Scott County, the political debate centered mostly on secession and rebellion. It seemed to Lester that whatever the eventual outcome, the practice of slavery would continue undisturbed.

Living like a hermit in the wild gave Lester little to do with his time but think, analyze, daydream, and anticipate. Each time he reflected on the home he was leaving, resentment toward the Southerners who caused this war was his inevitable reaction. In every seceded state it was the same – the wealthy planters fueled a hysteria that drove the South into a war that meant only trouble for Scott County and many more like it. All across the Deep South there were rallies, bands playing, preachers blessing the C.S.A., militias drilling, and adoration heaped on the boys who wore the uniform to take up arms in rebellion. Few wanted to miss out on the glory sure to be brought by a brief, triumphant clash with the Yankees. Now, six months since First Bull Run, the South watched as Mr. Lincoln built up his armies and navy for what portended to be a long, destructive war, one which would be impossible to stop after being so easy to ignite.

Hannah

The only family near Lester's home that he considered rich went by the name of Clifton. They had a thriving farm, a few slaves, and a house that stood out from most in the county. Still, travelers coming through would compare the Clifton place unfavorably with the grandiose manorial estates of the Cotton Kingdom. Whatever the Cliftons lacked in status or wealth, they compensated with arrogance and hypocrisy. The patriarch, Slade Clifton, was a self-important blow-hard who showed skill in inciting war but seemed to disappear whenever it advanced any closer than Murfreesboro. The son, Willard, gave the appearance of an overgrown juvenile at 22, with dreams that exceeded his abilities. He was currently enlisted in the Confederate force now occupying the Kentucky side of Cumberland Gap under the command of Brigadier General Felix Zollicoffer. The daughter, Hannah, was a delightful, genuine person who did not inherit any of the haughty, critical nature of Mrs. Ella Monroe Clifton. When Hannah was sixteen, her parents sent her to one of Nashville's most venerated private schools, but they must have been mightily disappointed when she returned home nothing like the delicate Southern belle they expected.

While gone, she had gained a broader perspective on the world, one that took her far beyond the backwoods of Tennessee or the pre-industrial South in general. Lester had known Hannah all the way through primary school and often walked her home before she went on to the higher levels. Lester himself had only completed the sixth grade.

Since going off to school, Hannah rarely came back to see her family. Lester wasn't sure why, but he sensed she never enjoyed being in Scott County. Then only a month or so ago, he saw her standing in front of the Huntsville post office. Lester recognized her at once, even though she had matured considerably while she was away.

"Maybe that fancy Nashville academy has made her into a high-falutin' snob like the rest of her family," he momentarily considered as he hesitated to approach her, mindful of his own social status.

He was still trying to decide what to do when Hannah's eyes fell on where he was standing and in a warm, cheerful voice she called out, "Lester? Is that my old school-friend? How are you?"

"I'm pleased that you remember me after so many years. Are you on vacation from school?" were the first words Lester stammered as he walked up to her.

"No, unfortunately, I had to return to Scott County because the war has upset everything in Nashville and the school had to close its doors. The city is a military installation now and no place for a young lady. I didn't really want to live in Scott County again, but I'm only nineteen and under my parents' control. At least I have the opportunity to teach school here," she added.

"You're a school-marm now?" Lester seemed surprised.

"I'm one of three in the grade school we attended together, more of a helper to the others, really. When I work with these young children, I have to feel sad that most will be stuck here in Scott County forever. It's even sadder that slave children will never know a better life than what they have now."

Lester asked her about her older brother, whom he hadn't seen in the area since secession.

"My brother Willard is in the Confederate army that's currently suppressing the local people who don't want soldiers here. He managed to get posted some distance from Scott County, where he's not popular. I hope you will be able to stay out of the army yourself."

Lester was tempted to ask, "Which side?" but in Eastern Tennessee, even a harmless joke could draw attention from the wrong people. Hannah invited him to sit with her on the bench in front of the building as they exchanged views on the issues of the day, mostly having to do with the war. The pleasant conversation was abruptly ended when Hannah was led away by her scowling, ill-humored father.

Jake

Even before Hannah expressed hopes for his safety, the idea of evading Confederate service had long occupied Lester's mind. He knew he would have to overcome the natural reluctance a man feels when it's time to leave home. He had earlier filled a knapsack with items most essential for survival and attached his bed-roll. When finally he summoned the courage, he disappeared into the deep forest. Now he was keeping his fire going and wondering what he'd do for food if Jake didn't show up soon. Jake was one of the slaves on the Clifton farm and the only person Lester had confided in. It was Jake who had first led him to this refuge and since then had been taking much risk by hiking two miles almost daily to bring food from the Clifton larder. At last he appeared about 3:00 with a sack of provisions slung over his shoulder.

"I brought you enough stuff to last you a few days, 'cause I think you should make your break for Kentucky now" were his first words as he plopped down by the fire. Before Lester could ask

"Why now?" Jake continued, "Union force under George Thomas hit Zollicoffer at Mill Springs, Kentucky, north of where we are now. Word is, Confederates broke and ran off in all directions. If they're scattered, maybe you can get through to Thomas's men."

Lester knew the area across the state line only a little, but when Jake mentioned the larger town of Somerset, he placed it north of the Cumberland River, near its confluence with the Big South Fork, which originates near Huntsville and flows north out of Scott County. The Fork would give Lester a route to follow through tortured terrain, but terrain that would make effective cover from detection. Once the route was decided,

Jake resumed, "Zollicoffer was killed in the battle and his boss, some general named George Crittenden, led the few men who didn't run on a retreat downriver toward Nashville."

This was the first time Jake had so much information to volunteer, so Lester asked where he had heard it. During war, all news is questionable. Jake told him matter-of-factly, "I read it in the newspaper when I went into Huntsville for the Clifton's mail."

It was against the law in most of the South to teach reading to slaves, so naturally Lester was curious how Jake had acquired literacy. "Miss Hannah was teaching me to read and write before she left for Nashville. Now she puts old books and things in a place where nobody else can find them. I think knowing how to read will be important if I ever hope to be free."

Lester exclaimed he was already benefitting from Jake's literacy, "If I reach Kentucky, it's because of what you read in a newspaper. Otherwise I wouldn't know where to go!"

"I been trying to learn what I can about this war. It's hard to do when I can't let anybody see me reading. The paper said the battle was fought on January 19. If it takes you a week to reach Mill Springs, I hope Thomas is still there," Jake stressed the urgency of departure.

Lester turned to the subject of Hannah's situation now that she was back in Scott County with guerrilla fighting swirling around the locale. Jake made it clear, "She doesn't want to stay here any longer than she has to. I think she's already had enough of the South."

"Maybe when this war is over, all three of us will be free to go where we want," Lester sighed, knowing it would be especially hard for Jake.

Kentucky was still a slave State and there was no safety for a fugitive. After sharing a few more thoughts, Jake announced he needed to make it out of the woods before dark. They wished each other well and parted with a firm handshake. As Jake hurried off along the route he was well familiar with, Lester knew he would miss the friend who had done so much for him. Now he would be on his own until he could reach the U.S. Army.

The fire was by now reduced to a bed of glowing embers, so Lester stoked it with the last of the firewood he had piled up during his nearly two weeks of cave-dwelling. A challenging, hazardous ordeal lay ahead and he had to sort through the information Jake had brought him.

Stretched out in the warm space between the fire and the cave wall, Lester had to wonder how many slaves in the South were as informed on the current situation as Jake seemed to be. Much of what Jake knew couldn't be found in newspapers. Lester hadn't pressed him for much more than he volunteered, but Jake had left him with the impression that more communication and knowledge were being shared among the slave communities than the Southern Whites wanted to believe. Lester understood from his own current situation that those in control, especially an uneasy control, worry most about people who know too much.

"I need to move out first thing tomorrow," Lester mumbled to himself as he went through his few options. "I have to do something to get out of Tennessee and this might be my only chance. I don't even know who will be there when I reach Kentucky.

The Mill Springs battle was fought five days ago. If it takes me a week to reach Thomas's camp, it puts me there in February. Nobody except Jake ever said much about George Thomas. All I know is he fought the first Union victory of the war over a collection of Rebels that probably included the Clifton son. If Thomas tries to advance through Cumberland Gap, the Confederates can move as many troops as they need into Knoxville now that the railroad bridges are replaced. For all I know, Thomas may be pursuing the retreating Rebels. Or maybe he's pulled back, but he'll never be closer than he is now."

Chapter 2
Off to Fight for Uncle Sam

The Big South Fork of the Cumberland flows through mostly unpopulated country marked by steep ridges, sandstone rock formations, ravines cut by creeks that run to the Fork, and thick undergrowth in places. There would be no trails to follow, so the only indicators of direction would be the Fork on his left and the clearings he had to avoid on his right. He would set out at first light in hopes of covering the fifty or so tortuous miles still in one piece. With the plan firmly fixed in his mind, Lester was able to sleep with no last-minute decisions to make in the morning.

An early start

The morning was chilly, but Lester bravely left the warmth of his blanket, secured his gear, and faced west, where he came upon the Big South Fork. The terrain presented every obstacle and barrier imaginable. Ravines with sides made slick by moss, huge boulders lying across his path, trees toppled by winter storms, thorny bushes – all made every day an exercise in exhaustion. Still, he kept covering ground, intent on reaching the Cumberland.

The weather had stayed mostly dry, so a warm, cheering campfire was one reward Lester could look forward to once he ended another day of hard-earned progress. One afternoon late, rain started falling and threatened to turn heavy, but it came while Lester was on dry land under a stand of pines that gave him some measure of shelter as he constructed a more water-repellent lean-to just large enough for sleeping.

Nature had eroded the land irregularly, sometimes creating natural arches that abound throughout the area and sometimes leaving a rocky point that Lester was able to scale. This was the only way he could gain some indication of his progress. From his first three vantage points, seeing the Fork to his left reassured him he was still going north, but his distance from the Cumberland was impossible to determine, especially since the convoluted route he had travelled added many miles to the trek. On the sixth day, Lester came upon a formation that looked like a colossal stack of pancakes created by a giant from six or seven flat rocks fifteen feet in diameter. It was an easier point to scale than the earlier ones, and soon Lester was rewarded with a clear view of the confluence with the Cumberland River, but it was too far away to make out any human activity. After descending, he crossed one more stream and found a canopy of pine boughs to camp beneath. He had gathered a few edibles in the woods, like nuts and roots that only a Cumberlander could identify, but tonight he ate the last of the morsels he had saved. He hoped he could reach the river in one more day, because he was sure to be hungry by then.

The country was a little more open now, offering frequent stretches of gentler terrain. In the late morning, Lester came upon a game trail that led through the trees. Scratched, bruised, mud-caked, aching, vile-smelling, nearly starved, he limped along, hoping to find Union pickets near the river. They should recognize him as one of the hundreds coming in from Tennessee to volunteer.

12-hour truce

Suddenly, Lester encountered a soldier who was equally surprised to see somebody else in this uninhabitable forest. The soldier was not wearing blue; it was that wretched butternut the Rebels used when they ran out of gray dye. Lester had come upon a tiny clearing when the Rebel sprang to his feet from where he had been trying to regain enough energy to move on. He was unarmed and Lester showed he was too. With no reason to do battle, the two sprawled out on the grass and leaves and they soon began relating their experiences of the past few days. The Rebel was named Raymond, from northern Alabama. He had served under Zollicoffer since the start in 1861.

"It don't take no Napoleon to see how bad our generals commanded at Mill Springs," Raymond began. "The reason I'm not armed is most of us were carrying smooth-bore flintlocks that belong in a museum. They sent us into battle during a heavy rain and most of our muskets failed to fire. When Zollicoffer was shot, Crittenden was worse than useless when it came time to run off in confusion. We left our wagons, artillery, horses, food, and camp equipage on the north bank of the Cumberland as we fled. Men were throwing down defective muskets and anything else that slowed them down in their flight.

Crittenden was drunk by that time and men are in no hurry to rejoin his ranks. All the martial airs and ladies blowing kisses didn't last us through the first week of soldiering."

"I was one of the last to be ferried across. The road on both sides of the river was littered with useless muskets and accouterments at first. Bayonets, cartridge boxes, and overcoats came next, and then discarded knapsacks and haversacks showed the panic in inexperienced troops fleeing like the devil was after them. I got the idea if I had enough food, I could survive as long as I had to in the rugged country closer to the fork. We figured Yankee cavalry would be coming down the road soon, but I kept looking through all the discarded haversacks for anything that was food. By the time I had as much as I could stuff into my knapsack and two haversacks, I was far behind the other stragglers. Somebody had dropped a .58 caliber Enfield. It was in top condition, but most of our cartridges were for a .69 smoothbore. I did find two minie balls in one of the haversacks and all powder is the same. Been livin' like an animal ever since. Had to stay on the west bank till the rain stopped long enough to let me ford the river. At home, I like to go squirrel huntin', but a fifty-eight would turn anything that small into mush. I seen this big old wild turkey up in a tree and I brought him down with one shot. I feasted on roast turkey for days. The last of my powder got soaked when I crossed the fork, so I had no more use for the Enfield. It's only a matter of time before Thomas's men patrol this side as well. If I can keep going east, the Confederate Army will report me as *missing* and assume I was drownded swimming the Cumberland as many did during retreat. When I reach safety somewhere, I can send my family a letter to say it ain't so."

"Where can you go that's safe? There's no safety anywhere in the country today," Lester wondered.

"I don't know what I'll do now. I can't go home to Alabama a deserter. If the Yankees catch me up here, I'm off to P.O.W. camp. I've heard plenty of talk in my regiment about the mountains in North Carolina and Georgia where anti-Confederates are organizing to encourage desertion and defection. Everybody knows Jeff Davis will start drafting men who don't have the money to avoid serving. Now there are anti-secession folks who are all set to ambush any Confederate soldiers trying to enter their refuge. Is that what it's like in Tennessee?"

"That's why I'm in Kentucky," Lester told him. "Scott County and most of the Eastern hill country is strongly Unionist. You have to pick a side – Rebel army or partisan guerrilla. It's a war within a war. If I have to fight at all, it will be in the U.S. Army."

Raymond nodded and added, "Seems like nobody in these parts wants to fight for the Confederates. The general who just clobbered us was George Thomas. He's from Virginia, so the North can't be too sure of his loyalty. I suppose that's why they put him in this God-forsaken backwater. One thing about this war – everybody is suspicious of everybody else, even in the same army. With so much confusion behind the lines, I don't expect the Southerners to support the rebellion when things start gittin' worse."

At this point, Lester remembered to ask for

information more important just then, "Do you know where the Union lines are? Do you think Thomas posted pickets this side of Big South Fork after Crittenden's skedaddle?"

The disillusioned butternut sighed with resignation, "There's a ferry landing not far from Mill Springs. Thomas is probably using our camps, where we built our winter shelters. We left him everything he needs for a comfortable stay."

Neither of the two had the energy or inclination to move on again that late in the day. The unofficial truce between a Union volunteer and a Rebel deserter made for a much-needed evening of resting weary bones and socializing. Raymond reached into his haversack and asked, "Hardtack?" as he handed a biscuit to a delighted Lester. "One of the haversacks I rummaged amounted to a bonanza. Take another one – and here's something to wash it down with," as he presented a good-sized flask. The whiskey was smoother than anything made in Scott County and the buzz was sublime. "They'll probably feed you when you reach Thomas's camps tomorrow. I wish I had snatched a blue infantry coat off the battlefield. Then I could head north and blend in with the scenery," Raymond ventured.

Lester chuckled, "With that *y'all drawl*, they'll take you for a Rebel spy and hang you."

"You'll fit right in with them Kentucky corn-crackers," Raymond smiled, faking indignation, and then quickly dozed off.

During the week-long trek, Lester had ended each day exhausted, his mind preoccupied with the singular goal of making it through this unforgiving terrain. He had seen the confluence the day before and according to Raymond, he was now close to Union lines. As Lester relaxed on the pile of leaves that served as a comfortable bed under the shelter of a mature evergreen, he was still trying to make sense of the confused state of this war he was about to enter.

He could hear Raymond's full-throated snoring, indicating a simple faith that the well-muscled Lester would do him no harm while he slept. "If we had been carrying muskets, would we still be sharing food, tobacco, whiskey, and personal information under truce?" he wondered.

Lester would soon learn that such fraternizing and trading between the lines was a common practice during a lull in the fighting. After this brief encounter with Raymond, he found it hard to imagine himself shooting at others like Raymond in battle.

"Neither of us could really explain why the armies are fighting in the first place. I'm joining the U.S. Army as the only way to escape the Rebels at home," he told himself. "Americans are killing Americans. Over what? The Davis government says it's for *States' Rights* while he sends his soldiers to trample the rights of Tennessee citizens. Lincoln wants to *Preserve the Union*, a union where even neighbors are fighting each other. No wonder both armies have forces scattered all over the map with no apparent purpose. Maybe it will make more sense when I reach Thomas's camp, but I don't even know about anything right here in Kentucky."

That was Lester's last thought before he finally dropped off to sleep. He would soon find Kentucky was a State (or Commonwealth) that geography had positioned between the two warring sides. The government in Frankfort had unrealistically issued a statement of neutrality, but then Confederate forces, without Richmond's approval, occupied and fortified the city of Columbus on the Mississippi. The violation of neutrality nudged Kentucky into remaining in the Union, though Kentucky continued to be represented by a star on Confederate flags. Lester had just entered another regional conflict, with both sides recruiting, training, and maintaining armies all across the state.

Camp on the Cumberland

The morning sun had cleared the horizon by the time Lester awoke, feeling restored from the extra sleep and eager to push on. Raymond had already left in his haste to avoid the very soldiers that Lester was hoping to find. The distance through the woods was still greater than he had planned on, but early in the afternoon, he decided he could make better progress if he were to veer right. He was sure there had to be a road that ran to the ferry landing. After a few more minutes in the trees, he came upon the wheel ruts of the primitive wagon road to the crossing. A person has to be careful in areas on the fringes of an occupying army. War attracts all kinds of bandits and bushwhackers who lurk in places where people are most vulnerable. He stayed right on the edge of the road near the woods until he could see the Cumberland River through the trees and two men in blue standing picket. He called to them from a distance and showed he was unarmed. To the pickets, he was just another refugee, so they asked him only the standard questions after he described the week-long ordeal he had endured to reach the Union Army. When Lester was asked, "Did you see any Rebels where you were?" he could not bring himself to betray Raymond. Besides, Raymond was deserting, so he was no longer a true Rebel.

"There's Rebels scattered all over between here and Cumberland Gap, but none that I saw near the river," Lester said with enough conviction that the pickets had no reason to question his loyalty.

Lester drew some satisfaction from having completed his solo campaign as the pickets had him escorted to the nearest camp, that of the 4th Kentucky Infantry regiment (U.S.). There he met regimental officers and staff with a confusing array of insignia, ranks, and functions. The quartermaster saw to it that Lester had an adequate uniform and rations. One of the aides took him through a small amount of enlistment paperwork, and then the chaplain gave him an inspirational talk that was mostly centered on the 4th Kentucky.

"The regiment was mustered in at Camp Dick Robinson during October 1861. Volunteers came in from about fifteen counties that represent a large area of eastern and northern Kentucky. Unlike units formed in a single town or county, most of the men came into camp as strangers to the rest. This diversity of origins can make it hard to establish esprit de corps. Kentucky as a whole is not a state with a single dominant culture, ruling class, or ideology. Much of the population relies on trade with the North along the Ohio River. Slave agriculture is practiced in the fertile tobacco and cotton regions toward the West.

On the other hand, few slaves are found in the Cumberland Plateau, and the high mountains have almost none at all. When you join the regiment, you'll think you're meeting men from every region of the state."

Four other privates invited Lester to join their campfire and soon he was feeling like a real soldier. His new messmates struck him as an interesting mix of characters. Despite their many differences, Lester could sense a strong bond forming among them during their first campaign. The 4th Kentucky was on the field when the fighting started and fought to the end in the battle that has been variously called *Mill Springs, Logan's Crossroads, Somerset, or Fishing Creek*. They had performed well under capable leadership and now were in high spirits. It was a good time for Lester to learn about army life and the military way of doing things.

There were no formal introductions when Lester took a seat by the fire. Civil War armies consisted mostly of citizen-soldiers away from their regular occupations and dispensed with ceremony. Since these volunteers were not professionally-trained career soldiers, the more successful officers respected the difference in adapting their command style. So far, the only officers' names Lester knew were Colonel Speed Fry, the regimental commander, and Brigadier General George Thomas, in command of the division now encamped at Beech Grove, across the river from Mill Springs.

The first soldier to welcome Lester was a young man named Jasper. He was the comic of the group who sometimes gave the appearance of being simple-minded. No matter how dire things may be, Jasper always had a joke to fit the situation. He claimed to have come from an isolated backwoods place near settlements called Rugless, Head of Grassy, and Awe, but nobody had ever heard of places like that. He was usually talking nonsense, but sometimes the nonsense would prove eerily prophetic. His first words to Lester were, "Ever had the measles?"

With Jasper, he was always looking for reactions, and he was taken aback when Lester showed none. Most of the population, in and out of the army, was well-aware of the contagious diseases sweeping through camps where men with no immunities were assembled from remote areas. Lester hadn't been told of the wave of measles that had recently afflicted Camp Dick, but the question didn't startle him.

"Why? Are you the camp carrier?" was Lester's nonchalant reply.

It was plain to see he was not a man easily ruffled and for the men in camp, this was important. One of the men who succumbed to measles before the start of the campaign was Jubal O'Grady. He had just become a mess-mate of these men who never really had the chance to know him. He had come from a landless family in the Rowan County backwoods and joined the Army for the pay. Jasper had also contracted measles, but managed to pull through after much suffering. Now he could turn it into a joke, his way of coping.

Gordon was next. He came from a rough neighborhood in Louisville and to the men he became *Grrr*, a comment on his disposition. He seemed to like the nickname, so it stuck. A stocky, muscular man who looked to be in his early twenties, he had been working on the loading docks along the Ohio River, so to him soldiering was a softer occupation and better-paying. Obviously of little schooling, Grrr tended to generate his own facts to justify his opinion on any issue. Then he would close is mind to anyone who differed. Still, he was likeable enough and promptly obeyed orders from his officers no matter what he thought of them. He asked Lester, "Where's your musket?" as if a new recruit would report already armed.

Muskets were stacked in a long line of teepees in front of a row of tents. "It's one of those," as Lester gestured toward them.

Grrr looked that way, hesitated, and continued, "I know where you can get one. Just look along the road to Monticello."

Raymond had told Lester during their truce about George Crittenden's chaotic retreat and Lester said he wanted to know more details.

"Is that where the Rebels went when they ran off?" he asked nobody in particular. "All's I know is what I learned from a deserter from Zollicoffer's brigade."

When it came to complicated matters and tedious analysis, the men deferred to Wilbur, the most book-smart among them. He was on the faculty at a college near Lexington and took a leave of absence when expectations were high for a short war. He was an idealist who vehemently opposed secession and told people he volunteered to show the sincerity of his convictions. That meant Wilbur was planning to run for political office. Like other volunteers, he had planned to return home triumphant after a few months, when he could tout his patriotic heroics. Now with no end in sight, Wilbur was stuck in the army. He could not even return home once his enlistment expired instead of reenlisting without people questioning the sincerity of his convictions.

Wilbur dutifully stepped into his classroom mode and began his battle synopsis. "Zollicoffer made his winter camp here, on the north side of the river. No general wants to fight with his back to a river he can't ford. Colonel Fry led us toward their camp and we were still some distance away when Zollicoffer advanced to meet us. More regiments came to the field on both sides as the fighting grew confused. Zollicoffer was shot when he mistook us for a Confederate unit and rode up to Colonel Fry before he realized his fatal error. Colonel Fry fired one of the shots, although he too was slightly wounded as he did. George Crittenden apparently ordered a retreat back to camp because they all fled the field. General Thomas directed artillery fire on the Rebel camp and the river was so swollen they panicked and left us everything, including these nice cabins and shelters. It's their food we're living on now. Good thing – the U.S. Army can't keep us supplied in this terrain. The Confederacy's most effective defense is the road system from here to the Gulf. That's the stage of civilization Dixie is in – the *Late Mud Age*. We've been slogging through mud all winter. The forty miles from Camp Dick took us eighteen days when we expected three."

"Does that mean General Thomas won't be taking us into East Tennessee?" Lester asked, already knowing the answer.

Wilbur turned even more cynical on the military

situation, "The Army of the Ohio is on its third commander already. The first was Robert Anderson, whose nerves were shot after his defense of Fort Sumter and he stepped down honorably. Then they replaced him with William T. Sherman, who's the brother of an Ohio senator. The Army sent him home after was judged insane. It was in the papers. Now Buell is in command in Louisville doing nothing."

After sitting silent and expressionless, the habitually gloomy and withdrawn Hubert made his first contribution to the conversation, "I guess that's the last we'll hear of Sherman. When will Lincoln send us somebody who knows what the hell he's doing?"

Hubert could always be counted on to make any matter seem worse. He came from a hog farm somewhere in the center of the state. Only 5' 4" in height, he had always been uneasy around people, insecure, and mostly a loner. He once intimated that his family urged him to enlist, presumably so he could gain some self-confidence, but he thought it was so they wouldn't have to feed him at home. When Hubert reported to Camp Dick in the previous October, he sulked and muttered to himself as if he was already sure he had made a big mistake.

"Now it's just as bad under Buell, who has five divisions wallowing in the mud while the Rebels build a line all across Kentucky," was his pessimistic assessment.

Before Hubert totally depressed everybody at the campfire, Wilbur calmly revived the conversation with a more learned approach. "I don't think General Thomas is urging Buell to send us through the Gap, but he'll go if ordered. I think he was ready and Buell pulled him back. Thomas knows how to fight, I guess. The Mill Springs battle was the first victory the North has won. Maybe by now, General Thomas has silenced all those who questioned his loyalty."

The 4th Kentucky would continue to serve in Thomas's chain of command for the rest of the war as he advanced through division, corps, and army command levels. The men in the Army of the Ohio had great affection for the general they called *Old Pap*.

The troops remained in camp until February 14. Their time was spent drilling, maintaining equipment, and finding fodder for the horses and mules. The hard slog from Camp Dick had taken its toll on draft animals and that made it even more obvious that the division's limited mobility precluded any major offensive operations into Eastern Tennessee.

Chapter 3
On Campaign in Central Tennessee

When the division broke camp, the troops began marching north, away from Cumberland Gap and toward Louisville. The men grumbled about how they had come all this way to fight a battle which they won handily, and in the end accomplished nothing. This was until they learned that the Mill Springs battle had unhinged the eastern end of the Confederate cordon across Kentucky. General Albert Sidney Johnston, Confederate commander in the West, had to withdraw forces from Bowling Green, Kentucky, which was now more vulnerable to an attack. He moved the troops to Fort Donelson, which had been constructed on the Cumberland River near the Kentucky-Tennessee line. The move did him little good. A Union force under Brigadier General U.S. Grant captured Fort Henry on the Tennessee River on February 6 and then compelled the *unconditional surrender* of Fort Donelson on February 16. Union gunboats now had complete mastery of the Tennessee River as far as Alabama, and the Cumberland as far as Nashville.

Nashville I: under occupation

Johnston withdrew from Kentucky altogether and soon had to abandon Nashville, which lay helpless before the Union gunboats. Since Nashville was in Buell's Department of the Ohio, his army had the honor of occupying Tennessee's State Capital without firing a shot. Thomas's division, after arriving in Louisville, was transported by water to Nashville on March 4. There, the 4th Kentucky went into camp until March 20.

Lester had remembered Nashville as a lively Southern city with conspicuous displays of wealth and economic prosperity. The streets had been full of citizens engaged in commerce and social activity against a backdrop of fine architecture in many public buildings and stately homes. That was all before Johnston evacuated Nashville, leaving the residents feeling betrayed as he consolidated his forces further south in Corinth, Mississippi. Some Confederate soldiers were so demoralized that many who lived nearby deserted rather than follow Johnston. The Confederates left to the residents most of the food they could not remove, but most who chose to remain in Nashville stayed inside their homes, fearing the worst from Yankee invaders about to arrive. On entering Nashville, soldiers described the city as looking empty and deserted.

Nashville had been an important production and distribution center for the western Confederacy. With the U.S. Army taking over the city for the rest of the war, it became a major base of operations and soon would be teeming with soldiers and civilians going in and out of its numerous warehouses, barracks, camps, hospitals, and shops where merchants were ready to sell their goods and services to the troops.

Lester was still footsore from the long days of

marching and he didn't mind the idleness and boredom of camp the way he would later as the war dragged on. Along with better footwear, he was provided with a .58 caliber Springfield rifled musket and the necessary accouterments.

He was enjoying the company of most of the men and didn't mind his new nickname *Mascot* as the only Tennessean in the regiment. Predictably, when the news reached camp that President Lincoln had appointed Andrew Johnson to the post of Military Governor in Nashville, the fact that he was from Eastern Tennessee didn't escape notice.

"Do they always grow them that short where you're from?" asked Grrr.

Lester told him, "He only looks short standing next to the President."

Jasper drew some chuckles when he suggested, "Try to imagine the short one as President."

Lester had been entertaining some faint hope that with Nashville occupied, Buell would come to the relief of the people in Eastern Tennessee, but the Army had other ideas. Buell was ordered to link up with Grant's Army of the Tennessee, which was in camp on the west bank of its namesake river at a place called Pittsburg Landing. The Union named its armies after the rivers that served their departments. The 4th Kentucky was in the Army of the Ohio, now two rivers away from where it started.

Too late for Shiloh

Transferring an army the size of Buell's could have been accomplished by river transports down the

Cumberland and up the Tennessee to Pittsburg Landing. For some reason, Buell chose to march all five infantry divisions cross-country through Columbia, Tennessee over 120 miles of primitive roads that were soon churned into trenches of mud by the marching troops, artillery trains, wagons, and mounted men. An army moving through rough terrain in hostile country beyond the reach of navigable waters can lose much of its strength before even seeing battle. The march was brutal, requiring twenty-two days to reach Grant's headquarters in Savannah, a pro-Union town on the east bank of the Tennessee, nine miles downstream from Pittsburg Landing. Hard rains and the inevitable bottomless mud wore down the men to the point where fatigue overcame so many that straggling was considered normal. Near the town of Columbia, the bridge over swollen Duck River had been destroyed and took much too long for engineers to replace. Since Thomas's division had recently seen combat, it was accorded a few more days of rest before being assigned the last position in the order of march. By this time, road conditions were at their worst for Thomas's advance.

On April 6, Thomas was close enough for the 4th Kentucky to hear the rumble of artillery from an unexpected battle being fought in Grant's camps. A night march was ordered when the alarmed Buell had to move in a timely manner to Grant's support. The physical demands went beyond the limits of endurance for some, who simply could go no further and dropped by the roadside. Nobody knew that a war could consist of exhausting marches, languishing in crude camps, and occasionally seeing the enemy.

Lester had not yet been involved in battle and it appeared he had dodged this one too.

Thomas's division remained on the east bank of the Tennessee during the action, while Buell's other four were engaged in the second day of the bloodbath that came to be known as the *Battle of Shiloh*. Thomas's division was ferried across to Pittsburg Landing on April 9 and sent into camps on the west side of the river. As the 4th Kentucky crossed, the landing came into view where two Union armies had disembarked only days ago. Those who had fought here had to be supplied, and soon they would be joined by even more.

Grrr was the first to react, "It's nothing but a mud-bank with room for about five of these scows. Nobody on the Louisville waterfront would work at a place like this."

One of the boatmen told him, "Shoulda been here on Sunday. There was hundreds of panicked recruits hugging this bank trying to get across to where you just come from. Made Grant's army look bad. The newspapers are always looking for gossip like this to print. You just wait."

Men in the camps of both Union armies wandered around the grounds, either hoping to find a relative in another camp or just out of curiosity. Lester and Wilbur decided to visit a regiment in Sherman's division that was camped in a field nearby. They had heard some exaggerated tales from Buell's men who fought on the second day and knew there had to be a different point of view. They had been hearing, "Grant's men were bayoneted in their tents," "Grant was drunk during the battle," "thousands of men fled at the first sounds of firing," "the whole of Grant's army had dissolved into fragments," "if we hadn't arrived when we did, he would have surrendered."

As they neared a group at their campfire, Wilbur cautioned Lester to be tactful when asking about the battle. "We're in the 4th Kentucky, Thomas's division. Did you men fight on both days?" Lester asked as he tried to project admiration for their service.

"We were on the right end of the battle line from the beginning. We held off the Rebs in front of our camps for some time before they threw in more brigades," said one man defiantly.

"Were any of your men bayoneted in their tents?" Wilbur tried to make it sound unlikely to be true.

"We were all up and in line of battle at the sounds of skirmish fire advancing from the other side of the woods. General Sherman was fired on as he personally rode to investigate while we formed up," was the emphatic reply of another soldier. "We were put into camp with hardly any training and got only a little before the attack. A number of men fled the field when the firing grew heavy, many of them crowding the landing. But some of them returned to their units and fought as hard as anyone on the second day, when we drove the Rebels back to Corinth."

Wilbur said he was puzzled over how Sherman returned to the Army after being called insane in the press. The same man told him, "He was rumored insane for claiming the Union would need 250,000 men in the West alone to put down the rebellion. Now we have nearabouts that many on the rivers already! Grant knew Sherman before the war and put him in command of our division."

Another added, "General Sherman was right there with us for the whole battle, even though several of his horses were shot under him. We saw him confer with Grant, who kept riding around the field directing the fighting. It did something for our confidence in fightin' back the poorly-organized Rebels. Much of our division stayed intact under Sherman. At the end of the day, he pulled us back into a strong line of defense that Grant had spent the afternoon preparing. We knew we could hold against anything the Johnnies had left to throw at us. We were glad to see the sun go down though."

A more critical soldier complained, "Johnston wouldn've attacked us at all if you Buell men had shown up when you were supposed to. Why the hell did you come all that way on foot?"

"I wish I knew," confessed Wilbur. "Maybe Buell thought we didn't get enough mud in Kentucky."

"Wilbur is the company mud authority," Lester crowed. "He can classify it by color, consistency, depth. He can even tell you the geological age when it was formed."

Another of Sherman's men related how the Rebels began the battle disorganized and continued to unravel through the day, making uncoordinated piecemeal attacks. "Over toward the river, Albert Sidney Johnston had to recklessly lead a charge into a hail of lead. It failed and Johnston was killed. We could tell when it happened because his Confederate units lost their cohesion and just shuffled around with no leader. This gave us the time we needed to strengthen our lines."

"Who succeeded Johnston?" Lester asked.

"Beauregard!" the man said.

"That's Pierre Gustave Toutant Beauregard," corrected another. "He's also called *Little Napoleon.*"

"In the East, they're calling McClellan *Young Napoleon*, and he hasn't even fought a real battle yet," offered Lester.

"Grant is the only general in the whole damned war who will fight!" bragged one of his more admiring men.

"If our army could lose Buell and put Thomas in command, we could fight as well as any army!" Lester argued. "But you're right; most generals seem too timid to make a move. No telling how long it will take us to move on Corinth!"

"If Grant leads it, it won't take no time at all," said the admirer.

Wilbur relayed accumulated gossip, "I hear Halleck is coming down from Saint Louis to take personal command. He's been fighting the war from his desk, but now he wants his share of the glory won by his field generals." This announcement bothered the Grant men more than a little.

Once in camp, Thomas's men were assigned to take part in burial detail. The ghastly landscape in areas that had seen the heaviest fighting was a sight Lester found horrifying. Many of the dead had not been moved from where they had fallen two or three days earlier, so the stench was overpowering. Lester had once been heartened by his messmates' accounts of battle at Mills Springs, but suddenly the reality of war's carnage was before him. This image would haunt him for as long as it took till the next tragedy to be inflicted by this war. The Union dead who could be identified were laid in marked graves, while unrecognizable bodies and Confederate dead were covered over in a burial pit as the only evidence of their time on earth.

"To the generals, these men will just be numbers on some casualty report. To their families at home, they are sons, husbands, fathers, and brothers. They didn't even know why they were killing each other except that they were ordered to," Lester muttered to himself as the last trace of enthusiasm for soldiering left him.

Casualties on both sides reached proportions never before approached in battles fought by American soldiers. Neither side had gained anything. The Southern people were forced to revise their expectations of a short, glorious war. The thousands of killed and wounded shocked the North as well, resulting in Union generals becoming even more conservative. The last half of 1862 did little to cheer either side.

The rumor that Halleck was taking command at Pittsburg Landing turned out to be accurate. When he arrived with his entourage, he remained true to his tendency of ceding the initiative to the enemy. Corinth, Mississippi was still Halleck's military objective, but he seemed to feel little urgency in taking it. Buell had already shown himself to be slow-moving, but now under Halleck, the pace became glacial. With a combined force more than twice the size of Beauregard's, he spent over a month digging, fortifying, and inching his way to Corinth. When the Federals reached the town, they found it abandoned. Beauregard's army had removed south to Tupelo, Mississippi.

The town of Corinth itself was not an impressive

prize. It consisted of a few dozen dingy structures, in this way resembling most towns in the South. The Confederates had considered Corinth essential to hold because it was built around the intersection of two major railroads – the Memphis and Charleston, and the Mobile and Ohio. When Memphis fell to the U.S. Navy a few days later, all of Western Tennessee was under Union occupation.

Halleck attached more importance to occupation than to directly confronting the enemy. Grant's army was consigned to occupation duty while Buell's was distributed along the Tennessee River as far east as a few miles from Chattanooga. The soldiers knew the strategic value of Chattanooga for any advance on Atlanta and access to Eastern Tennessee, but most knew its capture would require more than the feeble effort Buell was making.

Thomas's division was at first encamped at Iuka, Mississippi on the Memphis and Charleston Railroad just thirty miles east of Corinth. The men in the 4th Kentucky had plenty of time on their hands to grumble about their lack of confidence in high command. "Does anyone actually know what they're doing?" Hubert whined. "We're in the Army of the Ohio and most of us are on the Tennessee River. The Army of the Tennessee is on the Mississippi. Maybe Halleck lost his compass."

Wilbur added, "This is the time of year when Southern roads are dry enough to permit troop movement, our morale was high after Shiloh, and the Rebels are still reeling from their losses on the rivers. Yet here we are struggling along an inadequate railroad line."

"Maybe this is how Halleck plans to occupy Alabama – by controlling rivers and railroads," suggested Hubert. "Beats fightin'."

"It's senseless to occupy territory in the midst of a hostile population," Wilbur insisted. "As soon as the army leaves, they go back to rebellion. Halleck is too timid to fight, just like McClellan. Lincoln must be running out of patience."

Jasper wise-cracked, "Maybe he should put Halleck back behind a desk where he belongs!"

All agreed. On July 11, it was announced that Lincoln had ordered Halleck to D.C. as new general-in-chief. Though he still directed an ill-conceived strategy of occupation from his desk, he was too distant to meddle in field operations.

Chapter 4
Disunity in Dixie

Buell found it took time to establish a line of supply to sustain a large army strung out along the Alabama segment of the Tennessee River. The long delay gave the soldiers a chance to observe conditions on the Southern home front. Few of the Kentucky men had ever been this far South before, but now they could see how war was bringing its hardships closer to the civilian population. One night, Lester mentioned he had just heard some Rebel deserters had come into camp. "They brought some surprising stories about reaction to the Confederate draft. I hear tell there's not much liking for the Davis people."

Wilbur added, "Richmond passed the conscription and impressments act a week after the Rebel losses at Shiloh. That shows how short-sighted they were about their ability to carry on a long war. Wars always last longer than planned."

"That's how they are!" Impulsive! They don't worry about consequences," Jasper echoed the stereotype that prevailed in the North.

"Jasper, yer right this time!" seconded Lester. "Richmond must have thought Southerners wouldn't notice how the act favors the privileged, like the rich planters. Anybody between ages eighteen and thirty-five is supposed to fight for the cause for three years, but if they have the money, it's easy to get an exemption. They can hire substitutes or pay off officials who create imaginary positions they claim are critical to the rebellion. But then soldiers come and take a poor man away from his hungry family. "

"Plus, Davis extended all one-year enlistments to three," Wilbur noted. "Next it's only a matter of time till they draft even younger and older men."

Hubert weighed in, "The men in an Indiana regiment said a family of poor refugees came in yesterday. They said impressment agents showed up and took everything the family had – horse, livestock, meat from the smokehouse, cornmeal, flour, sugar. They even raided their vegetable garden. The same thing happened to their neighbors. All the while, the planters don't pay, since they're not growing food crops."

Grrr pointed out, "The Confederates have been using their slaves to labor on their fortifications."

"Yeah, and all that does is make it easier for them to escape," Jasper countered. "Someday Lincoln will order the generals to welcome them into our lines."

"If Lincoln does that, be prepared for a whole flood of runaways from anywhere near our position. Combined with the white refugees, we'll be feeding half the population down here," Hubert muttered.

Buell's advance up the Tennessee Valley was barely sputtering along. Thomas's division was ordered to Tuscumbia, Alabama, on the south side of the river. There, it remained through most of July. Soldiers began to wonder if Buell understood the concept of *time*.

Thomas's camp at Tuscumbia was near that of

Alexander McCook. General McCook was one of the celebrated *Fighting McCooks of Ohio*, who consisted of two brothers and their sons, fourteen in all. The drudgery of camp life, along with short rations, led to a restlessness that caused some men to wander randomly through the thousands of tents that covered every available patch of level ground. Wilbur, always on the hunt for diversion, was moseying through an area near the camp of a Minnesota regiment. He greeted some soldiers who were talking with an excitable Ohio private from McCook's division. Like Wilbur, Private Hutchins was walking off the boredom. When he told these Minnesota boys he was from McCook's division, they began asking him questions about the experience on Day 2 of Shiloh, which they had been spared. He was still noticeably agitated and didn't want to revisit that day, so he shifted the topic to why they were bogged down in Northern Alabama. "When do we get moving again? Is Buell taking our whole army to Chattanooga?"

As the talk continued, it seemed to Wilbur that Hutchins was oddly uninformed on matters that were common knowledge in camp days earlier. Wilbur had spent some of his early life in Ohio, so he knew the state well.

"Where was your regiment mustered in?" he asked in the least skeptical-sounding tone possible.

"I enlisted at Camp Corwin in Dayton," Hutchins seemed to be reciting from memory. "Just north of Cincinnati."

"Is that where your family lives?"

"On the edge of town."

"How far from the Cuyahoga River?" Wilbur had

attended college in Hiram, Ohio near Cleveland, where the Cuyahoga River actually flows.

"Not far at all. Just a little East," he sputtered, turning to distance himself from the inquisitive Wilbur.

Other soldiers who heard the exchange also grew suspicious. Just as Hutchins thought he was a safe distance from the conversation, another asked him, "When do you report back to Tupelo?"

"In two days, I gotta…." Hutchins, or whatever his name, realized he had just betrayed himself. As he was being escorted to the Provost Marshall, he pleaded to tell anything he knew if it would save him from the firing squad. That night the men listened for a volley of four or five muskets anywhere near camp, but there were no signs the Rebel spy had met his maker that soon.

The reported rate of desertion from the Confederate army made for lively discussion in the camp of the 4th Kentucky. The draft act led not only to an increase in the number of Southern men deserting the ranks, but desertion was not as widely condemned in many areas of the South. Deserters and layouts controlled inaccessible places in mountains and swamps, towns, and even whole counties. It seemed that the lively spirit of defiance and independence that pervaded the South at the start of the war was running low in parts of Dixie. It was not hard for Union soldiers to understand the demoralizing effects this war was producing in the Rebel soldiers. In the U.S. Army, campaigning was plenty difficult, but at least their families were safe, the food adequate, and they had won some battles. Fighting a war with inferior materials and shortages plus anxiety over home and family had to weigh on Johnny Reb. He had to figure it would just grow worse in the South. Northern industry was experiencing great expansion while the war was slowly impoverishing and starving the Southern people.

Grrr couldn't wait to announce what he said must be true because he heard it from somebody who lives in the area. "He said only the folks with the most slaves wanted to secede. But they control everything in government, so they start a war where everybody else fights so they can keep their slaves. The folks here are saying it's a *rich man's war and a poor man's fight*."

This was not really news to anyone in camp, though they knew the issue was more complicated than Grrr's statement would suggest. Naturally, Wilbur thought the subject needed elaboration and the group needed his perspective on Southern society.

He began, "Most wars are fought that way. Down here, the social structure just makes it easier to send others to fight for them. The Southern aristocracy has been trying to imitate the feudalism of medieval Europe for generations. The cotton kingdom plantations are nothing more than the manorial estates from the days of Sir Walter Scott. You'll see that if we ever get that far South. They try to be self-sufficient, trade by barter and credit, and get most of the artisan work done by slaves. Have you seen many prosperous towns in the South, with stores, banks, craftsmen, schools, liveries, tailors, or apothecaries? The yeoman farmers and poor whites depend on planters for things like loans, ginning their cotton, grinding meal, repairing tools, shoeing horses, the kind of things that Northern farmers find in town. Anything the planters need used to come from Europe or the Northern States before the blockade. The poor whites have to hand-fashion stuff we can buy in stores. The planter class has the political power to control government in their own interests. They keep taxes low, so education and transportation are primitive. Look at their roads; people have to be good horsemen just to wade through the mud."

"Again, the mud expert!" Jasper interrupted as others went into a conspicuous fit of yawning. Mud was still the one feature of this war that irked Wilbur and he voiced his displeasure daily. He continued in his role as camp expert on things other than mud.

"The whole structure depends on maintaining slavery. The planters fear it will be similar to how it was in Europe when serfdom ended and the nobility lost its importance."

"Why don't the poor stop fighting for the privileged? That way, they'd give up on war with the North," asked Hubert, still trying to find hope for a path to a short war.

"It can't happen here," Wilbur ruled. "The Southern Whites are united on one thing – fear of a slave uprising. That fear was heightened by the John Brown raid. Then they learned it was instigated by a Northerner. That's why the civilians down here shudder when we march through their home-front singing 'John Brown's Body.' Most families don't even keep slaves, but think the institution of slavery is the only way to control them. Even most of the Unionists down here don't want to see Emancipation upsetting the status quo. There's talk about Davis exempting one overseer for every twenty slaves on a plantation."

Hubert looked puzzled, "How could the slaves possibly revolt when there's no way to arm them? Aren't the Confederates just wasting men when they keep them back from the lines?"

"They are." Lester nodded. "Even before I left Tennessee, I could tell the slaves knew more about the war than most folks think. In fact, I'm pretty sure slaves are already helping us without raising suspicion."

"Like how?"

"Things like scouting the best routes through the country, location of the enemy, where to find forage, things like that."

"What do we have to do before the common folk will stop supporting the war?" asked Grrr, whose disdain for any sort of ruling class was always on display.

Wilbur tried to describe how he viewed the military situation, "This is not like war in Europe with two armies contesting a national border with loyal populations behind them. Maybe European warfare is what the generals learned at West Point, but it doesn't work over here. There's fighting going on all across the map and there aren't enough soldiers in the world to man a line stretching from Kansas to the Atlantic. We take a few towns, post a garrison, and try to patrol the immediate vicinity. There's no telling what lies beyond until you reach the Confederate-controlled frontier. The no-man's land in between is not safe for anyone when civil authority breaks down. Inhabitants are visited by foragers, guerrillas, and armed bandits.

Sometimes deserters gang up to ambush cavalry sent to bring them in. No wonder so many starving White refugees are showing up in towns we garrison. I hear that fugitive slaves are coming into Grant's camps and he's not turning them away."

The slow advance up the valley to Chattanooga was becoming a logistical nightmare. The drought that was afflicting much of the South brought down the water level in the Tennessee River to where it was too shallow for navigation of supply vessels. Buell had to depend on railroads that were always vulnerable. The Memphis and Charleston Railroad experienced repeated acts of sabotage by Rebel irregulars. To the north of Buell's army, the railroads between Louisville and Decatur were heavily damaged by cavalry under Nathan Bedford Forrest and John Hunt Morgan. Men in the U.S. infantry had little regard for the value of U.S. cavalry to begin with, and now they cursed its inability to protect the supply lines when the men went down to half-rations and were unable to find forage in this cotton-growing valley. Soon after Thomas's division reached Decatur, the men learned that the campaign for Chattanooga had to be abandoned. A major Confederate invasion of Kentucky was underway.

Halleck was still practicing his ineffective strategy of occupation while the Rebels were conducting an offensive campaign to bring Kentucky into the Confederacy. It was genuinely believed that thousands of Kentuckians would flock to the banners of a *liberating* Confederate army. Wagons carrying twenty thousand muskets accompanied the invaders to arm the eager volunteers.

The offensive involved two independent forces that entered Kentucky by separate routes. In March of 1862, Major General Edmond Kirby Smith was made the latest in a succession of Confederate commanders in Eastern Tennessee. He showed even more hostility toward the Unionists than his predecessors as partisan violence intensified. In August, he led his troops across the Cumberland Mountains and reached Lexington that same month. A much larger force, soon to be labeled the *Army of Tennessee*, had been regrouping in Tupelo since losing possession of Corinth. Its new commander was Braxton Bragg, whose unpopularity with the men and fellow generals would turn to near-mutiny over the next year. Though Kirby Smith held an independent command, Bragg agreed to join him in Kentucky. While Buell was still in Alabama, Bragg's army moved by a roundabout rail route and won the race to Chattanooga. From there, Bragg marched his men across the Cumberland Plateau in the direction of Louisville. Only local militia and volunteer units were present to defend Louisville and Cincinnati until Buell's army could arrive.

Self-emancipation

On July 24, Thomas's division began moving north to join in the pursuit of Bragg. The men in the 4th Kentucky were leaving Alabama wondering whether the months spent between Corinth and Decatur had amounted to any good. They had managed to antagonize some previously pro-Union citizens and turned their backs on fugitive slaves who were hoping to follow the army to freedom. Buell, like many in his ranks, thought of the slaves only in terms of a hindrance to his military operations. Such treatment was now against regulations, since that same month U.S. Congress passed its *Second Confiscation Act*, which expanded the designation *contraband of war* to apply to slaves coming into Union lines. The generals could not return them, but treatment of the newly-free was uneven and sometimes reached levels of inhumanity.

The exodus of slaves to the U.S. Army was triggered by the Confederate generals who used impressed slaves to labor near Union lines. The first few who escaped and were not returned led to a flood of families and individuals seeking freedom in the U.S. camps. Word had spread through the network that came to be known as the *grapevine telegraph* during the war. The Army was not prepared for this influx, but soon camps were constructed near garrisoned towns like Memphis, Corinth, and La Grange. Called *contraband camps*, they continued to spring up in numerous sites from North Carolina and Arkansas.

With better standards came charity groups that worked with the Army to establish schools, orphanages, and hospitals. When nearby plantations were abandoned by fleeing owners, they could be operated by Northern businesses to provide paid employment to the new arrivals.

The mix of attitudes held by men in the 4th Kentucky was typical of the border states in that era. Some soldiers were outright racists who wanted no army involvement in emancipation, a sentiment shared by some generals. But Lester noticed that more than a few soldiers were disturbed the first time they witnessed the inhumanity that formed the basis of the plantation system. Southerners had always contended that slavery was a benign institution and the chattels were content with their lot. That claim was hard to reconcile with the masses of people who were risking their lives for an uncertain future when blue-clad armies came near. Southern planters came to be objects of disdain to the U.S. soldiers who were marching through the South.

By the time Buell put Thomas in motion North from Decatur, Bragg was already near the Kentucky line. More time was consumed when Buell consolidated all of his divisions in Nashville before continuing his pursuit of Bragg. Thomas's division remained in Nashville between September 8 and 15. When the division left Nashville, Kirby Smith was in the area of Lexington while Bragg had entered Glasgow, east of Bowling Green. Buell directed his army to Louisville, which he presumed to be Bragg's objective. Lack of water during this season made for a grueling march. A stagnant pool in an otherwise dry streambed could be cause for celebration and even battle. The thousands of volunteers that were expected to join the Confederacy never showed up. The two Rebel forces were still operating independently and both commanders were uncertain as to where Buell's divisions were concentrating. Kirby Smith put the scare into Cincinnati, but thousands of civilian volunteers rallied behind barricades and discouraged the Rebel scouting party from coming as far as the Ohio River.

Bragg blundered into part of Buell's army in the *Battle of Perryville*, near the Kentucky town of the same name, and the major battle of the campaign ensued on October 7-8. Thomas was positioned some distance from Perryville and did not reach the battlefield. The battle was inconclusive, but two days later, Bragg met with Kirby Smith and the two concluded there was insufficient food and fodder in Kentucky to sustain the offensive. They agreed to return to Tennessee by way of Cumberland Gap, still encumbered by twenty-thousand muskets that had found no takers. Kirby Smith resumed his role in Knoxville while Bragg continued on to Chattanooga, and then took possession of Murfreesboro, twenty miles southeast of Nashville.

President Lincoln was disappointed in Buell's failure to pursue Bragg's army in retreat. He lost his patience with generals too slow or too timid. This meant both Buell and McClellan had to go. Buell was replaced by William Rosecrans and Ambrose Burnside was appointed to replace McClellan. Rosecrans had enjoyed some success in small battles, and Lincoln was willing to try him in command of a large army. Rosecrans's first action was to reorganize his divisions in Nashville. Since he made his headquarters in Nashville, his army was renamed "Army of the Cumberland."

Nashville II: Refuge in a desolated land

The city's appearance had changed since Lester's regiment marched out six months earlier. He had already seen its transformation from a vibrant antebellum Nashville to the stunned city that Albert Sidney Johnston had abandoned in February. Since then, it had gained a large, noticeably diverse population, but few seemed to be enjoying the experience. The Army had constructed fortifications that discouraged any offensive approach by land. The occupying force had Nashville under control and tolerated little disorder. Refugees, contrabands, Confederate deserters, or orphans did not care what side of the war others were on. Most were concerned with their own survival.

Garrisoned towns offered some measure of security and stability to swelling populations. The military government established police, fire companies, health care, and a court system. Food and other essentials were provided to the destitute. Churches, schools, and markets remained open. Nashville was now a major military base in need of civilian workers, so there were jobs for the willing. As more and more of Tennessee came under Union control, other towns were similarly garrisoned, but little could be done for people in no-man's land outside the Army's protection.

Hostility and resistance to Union occupation among the inhabitants of Nashville convinced Rosecrans that softer controls were not working. He imposed harsher restrictions and required loyalty oaths with considerable penalties for violating either. These included seizure of property (called *sequestration*), imprisonment, and banishment.

Lester's regiment was put into winter camp on January 13, 1863 at Lavergne, just outside of Nashville. Once ensconced in a camp that the soldiers made as comfortable as they could, Lester and his comrades had the chance to reflect on the landscape they had just crossed between the Tennessee River and the Ohio. Since Perryville, the 4th Kentucky had been assigned to provide infantry support to cavalry troops in trying to chase down the Confederate raider John Hunt Morgan. In this, the cavalry was unsuccessful, as Morgan continued his destructive raids that even reached into Indiana and Ohio.

The widespread desolation inflicted on their home state understandably embittered men in the 4th Kentucky. Conversation in camp centered on the countryside left scarred and barren by repeated visits from raiders, regular cavalry, marching armies, foragers, and guerrillas.

"We will be seeing that anywhere we go from now on," prophesized Wilbur. "The movement of armies through areas like this always begins the process of devastation. Once they go somewhere else to fight, they leave behind a population vulnerable to the worst kind of lawless and desperate bands that range across the countryside at will. In some places where the armies are not near, all civil authority breaks down and anarchy rules. If our generals ever get us moving further south, the territory in our wake will quickly descend into disorder."

Lester added, "We saw this in Tennessee as we came up from Alabama – People losing their crops, their homes. If that starts happening in other parts of the South, the Confederacy will destroy itself from within."

Wilbur was quick to tell him, "Anywhere no troops are present, it's already happening. Parts of Mississippi,

Arkansas, and Missouri are crawling with various irregulars and outlaw bands."

"So why are we even fighting this war?" Hubert whined. "All we do is bring ruin wherever we go. It seems there has to be a better way of preserving the Union than by destroying half of it."

"If I knew how, I'd be President," smiled Wilbur. "The Rebels will keep fighting the war until the whole South is in ruins. But I think generals like Halleck and his lackeys will still consider holding key positions the basis of strategy."

"Aren't we starving out the Confederacy?" Grrr seemed confused. "Isn't the blockade of ports like Charleston and Mobile working?"

"If we had another ten years, it might work. But even with the blockade tightening, they'll hold out until the Lincoln administration runs out of support. The generals have to find a faster way to end the rebellion," Wilbur insisted.

"Meanwhile, what do the generals do to keep Morgan and Forrest off our supply lines?" Jasper wished someone would tell him. "Cain't we get more cavalry to protect the railroads?"

"You can't just create a cavalry unit from scratch. It takes longer to train a cavalry trooper than to train the horse." Wilbur showed what he was picking up from talking with officers.

The U.S. Cavalry that did exist in the Western theater was not being effectively used by any of the early generals. Infantry men never eased up in their derision of the cavalry that could not protect lines of supply and communication. Rosecrans was finding it hard to meet the enormous supply needs of both his army and the swelling civilian population of the Nashville vicinity. The water level of the Cumberland River was still too low for navigation, so he was wholly dependent on the railroad from Louisville.

While in Nashville, Rosecrans consolidated his infantry into three *wings* that soon came to be called *corps*. The 4th Kentucky would be serving in XIV Corps under George Thomas, the division of John Brannon, and the brigade of John Croxton.

By the time Lester and the 4th Kentucky returned from their pursuit of Morgan, Rosecrans's army had fought a bloody encounter with Bragg at Murfreesboro between December 31 and January 2, 1863. The town stood squarely in the path of any advance on Chattanooga. Built on the west bank of Stone's River, it was served by the Nashville and Chattanooga Railroad. The intense battle is known as *Stone's River* in the North and *Murfreesboro* in the South. The casualty count shows it to be the bloodiest battle of the war in terms of killed and wounded as a percentage of total numbers engaged. Like so many other battles, this one served no purpose for either Rosecrans or Bragg, and since the inevitable outcome was Bragg's withdrawal south, it could have been accomplished without costing Bragg thousands of men the Confederate Army could ill-afford to lose. Rosecrans still had the goal of capturing Chattanooga, but he insisted on remaining in Murfreesboro for six months. Bragg's army went into winter camp near the town of Tullahoma, between Murfreesboro and Chattanooga.

The other main armies were also immobilized by winter road conditions in the South. The Army of the

Potomac was on its fourth commander – Joe Hooker, who took command after it ground to a halt during Burnside's *Mud March*. On the Mississippi, Grant was mired in the delta and bayous trying to put a land force on dry ground outside of Vicksburg. Nothing could move until spring.

A powerful ally

Going into 1863, the Confederacy was still defending most of its original territory, though at horrific cost in men and resources. The free Southerners at home were suffering in this war, but still – at least outwardly -- hopeful and enduring the hardships with men away from home, poor harvests, impressments, and banditry. To criticize the *Cause*, as it came to be known throughout the South, could still be considered treason. The hope was that England would recognize the sovereignty of the Confederacy and push for a peaceful separation. The people of the North were losing patience with armies that seemed to be making no progress in a war that was not universally popular to begin with.

The dawn of 1863 did not signify a resounding military triumph, but it marked a radical and controversial shift in President Lincoln's prosecution of the war. The final version of the *Emancipation Proclamation* became effective on this New Year's Day. As expected, the effects were widespread and profound in matters diplomatic, political, military, and moral. The President was an astute lawyer who crafted the Proclamation as a military order issued by the Commander-in-Chief to officers of the U.S. Army and Navy. Slavery was still protected under most interpretations of the Constitution, which the President had sworn to uphold, so the Proclamation was worded to give it legal justification.

The Proclamation sent tremors through the South. Davis and others condemned it in hateful language. Most slaves saw it differently, as the grapevine carried information to many thousands who were newly emboldened to escape into U.S. lines. The many who could not flee were finding ways to assist Union armies and weaken the Confederacy from within. A South already finding it hard to grow sufficient food or produce needed goods was not helped by a labor scarcity or slow-down. In some cotton-growing areas, slaves outnumbered Whites, causing a sense of dread over the prospect of insurrection. Planters had been removing slaves to areas far from railroads and rivers to keep them from impressments agents or Union forces. The practice was called *refugeeing* and was especially tragic to the many thousands sent all the way to Texas when the Mississippi River was still in Confederate control.

Lester's regiment mirrored the mixed reactions to Lincoln's Proclamation in the Northern States. The men had volunteered in order to preserve the Union, not to free slaves. For many soldiers, anxieties provoked by the Proclamation centered on what its provisions meant for them individually. Few had read it, but all had had their own opinions. Soon after the 4th Kentucky went into camp, Grrr announced he had just heard that the slaves in Kentucky were all immediately free after New Year's Day. Few believed him, but he remained inflexible. As debate extended into the meaning of other provisions, Jasper suggested that Wilbur would probably delight in being consulted.

"He's trying to be a politician, so he must be collecting all the news he can about stuff like this," Jasper reasoned.

Wilbur could be seen lately circulating through the brigade's camps and speaking with the officers to the point of their annoyance. The next time he returned to his own camp, he welcomed the chance to conduct a spontaneous seminar. It seemed to Lester that some soldiers wanted just enough information to keep arguing without conceding any points. Understandably, the Kentucky men were most concerned with the immediate effect on Kentucky, where slaves made up twenty percent of the population. As expected, Wilbur began in his best classroom voice, "Since the Proclamation applies only to *States or parts of States* considered to *be in armed rebellion*, Kentucky and other border states are exempted. But if you ask me, slavery is going to die out anyway, unless we give up on fighting the war."

"So we can free the slaves in Tennessee, but not in Kentucky?" gloomy Hubert protested.

Wilbur was undeterred in demonstrating his intellect to the Kentucky farm boys and hill people, "Tennessee is exempt too, because we occupy more than half the State and run the government in Nashville."

Lester muttered something about still needing to occupy Eastern Tennessee before Hubert went on, "So we fight here so a rebellious state can come back in with its slaves?"

Wilbur saw how the particulars could be confusing, so he went in a new direction, "Who can tell? The longer the war goes on, the harder it will be for the South to return to its old ways. It may be already too late. The whole system that depended on slavery was obsolete before the war started. The rest of the world has left the South behind."

Hubert still complained, "If Lincoln means to free only slaves in enemy-held territory, his proclamation is just a piece of paper."

"Sometimes in government, a piece of paper can accomplish what armies can't," Wilbur the politician confidently stated. "By making Emancipation a military goal, Mr. Lincoln is implying the Confederacy is fighting to preserve an institution that is growing unpopular in most parts of the world. This discourages diplomatic recognition, especially from England."

As soon as Wilbur wandered off to another camp, probably to pester more officers, talk in the 4th Kentucky degenerated into rumor, opinions, and anecdotes, most having to do with the recruitment of liberated slaves to serve in the Army and Navy. Some doubted that after knowing nothing but forced servitude, men could be suddenly expected to act as an organized unit or even take care of themselves without supervision.

"An organized unit?" Jasper interjected. He had no opinion; he just wanted to change the subject to one he found more interesting. "Ever hear what the men who fit at Shiloh and Stone's River say about Rebel units in battle? They can't keep any organization once they go in. Our infantry keeps a tight formation, but with the Johnnies, it's every man for himself, like they're racing to see who gets shot first. They put all their energy into one desperate charge. And with that hideous Rebel yell, they're out of breath before they hit our lines."

Grrr had it all figured out. "That's because Southerners were never used to taking orders. In the South, only slaves take orders. The officers find it hard to command them unless they lead personally from the front. That's why so many of their generals are killed in battle. Albert Sidney Johnston was shot at Shiloh while leading a charge on horseback 'cause he couldn't get one of his brigades to move forward."

"What should they do?" Hubert wondered. "I hear at Antietam, McClellan made his headquarters so far back from his lines that he could not follow much of the action."

Lester mentioned his conversation with some of Grant's men right after Shiloh. "They told me and Wilbur that soldiers on the front line drew much strength from knowing he was with them in the thick of battle. To see their commander a few feet behind the line, calmly issuing orders while chomping on his cigar, gave them confidence that he had everything under control; there was never a look of crisis or urgency on Grant's face."

"How do his men like it now that he's actively pushing for recruitment of U.S.C.T. regiments?" wondered Grrr. When Jasper looked confused, Grrr added, "That's *U.S. Colored Troops*."

"Grant announced they will be a *powerful ally*, but generals can't even agree on the issue," said a voice the men recognized as belonging to Wilbur before he stepped into the glow of the campfire. "Most of them think they'll strengthen the Army by serving garrison duty but don't want to send them into combat. They fear a major negative reaction among the troops. Just the announcement itself caused a wave of desertions in other Border State regiments."

Racism could be found all through ranks, but the Army was feeling heat from Washington politicians. The Republican Party had fared poorly in the 1862 Congressional elections and power was shifting toward the Peace Democrats. Some of these were labeled as traitors by the Radical Republicans, leading soldiers to resent elected officials who were waving the white flag in a year when few soldiers were permitted by their states to vote by absentee ballot. Rosecrans himself entertained political ambitions that favored siding with Lincoln's party. He even transferred out some officers who were vocal anti-abolitionists. By this time, more soldiers were accepting the military necessity of emancipation, and some even liked the feeling of marching in a liberating army.

Nashville III: A Northern city

After nearly a year of continuous Union occupation, Nashville had become a major military installation, recruiting center, and transportation hub. The swelling civilian population required relief and services from the Army, civil government, and private charities. Mixed in with the arriving refugees were smugglers, spies, prostitutes, and assorted petty criminals. Sickness and violent crime added to the misery afflicting so many in the camps. For the Union occupiers, keeping order could be difficult duty. There were still defiant secessionists, despite the harsh penalties.

The observation Wilbur had made about slavery being effectively finished in Tennessee seemed to be ringing true. Despite its exemption from the Proclamation, citizens realized slavery could not be sustained. By the end of the war, twenty thousand African-American volunteers will have enlisted from Tennessee in exchange for the promise of freedom. Nashville was becoming a major center for organizing U.S.C.T. volunteers.

When Lester was permitted to walk through Nashville, he wished he could find Jake somewhere, but that was unlikely. With Confederates in control of the upper valley, he could never make it out to the closest Union forces. Hannah stood a better chance, since her father was a well-known secessionist. To the occupying soldiers, Slade Clifton was just a windbag few took seriously, but his devotion to the Confederacy made him a harmless nuisance. Still in awe of the heavy military activity all around Nashville, Lester put more purpose into his stroll, one that found him visiting shelters, camps, orphanages, hospitals – anywhere he might find a familiar face from Scott County.

Lester had been told some time ago that he had relatives in Nashville, but he had never met them and knew only that his mother's maiden name was *Duncan*. It was hard to find anyone in the city who had been living there before the war, and nobody with any knowledge wanted to talk to a Yankee invader. After walking several blocks, he stopped to talk with a tailor who told him there was *a Duncan Apothecary* a few doors down the street. When Lester entered the shop, he met an amicable fellow who bore no family resemblance. Even so, the druggist turned out to be Cyrus Duncan, his mother's cousin. He reported the family in Knoxville was still safe as long as they did nothing to antagonize the Confederates.

"The Confederate regulars are behaving more like guerrillas now. Union partisans in turn get more violent. Civilians can't travel in and out, with Rebel soldiers guarding the train depots. Civilians need papers issued by authorities to go anywhere."

"How long has the railroad been controlled like that in Knoxville?" asked Lester.

"It began when Kirby Smith replaced the dead Zollicoffer. After he crossed into Kentucky, the troops he left to hold Knoxville took total control of the railroad traffic. One officer was severely reprimanded when he allowed a young lady who looked like a plantation belle board the train with her personal servant, who was loaded down with her baggage. She must have had connections or something."

Lester reacted to this news, "The lady – was she from Scott County?"

"Can't say. Since Nashville fell in 1862, we've been seeing folks come in from all over Tennessee and a few manage to escape the upper valley. They're all praying for Northern forces to come to their relief," Cousin Cyrus said, as if expecting some information.

Lester could only say, "We can't do anything till we take Chattanooga. That's not easy in this winter weather."

Mr. Duncan had no further information that Lester needed, but he told his new-found cousin he was welcome to check with him again next time his unit was near. Lester thanked him for the report on his mother's situation in Knoxville and left the shop feeling less anxiety over that. Still, he had spent half the day in Nashville with little else to show for it. The description of a young lady at the Knoxville depot could fit any number of Tennessee debutantes. If indeed Hannah had reached Nashville, where would she have gone? She wasn't likely to be serving in any military function, but she may be ministering to the sick or engaged in teaching refugee children. Nashville's contraband camps continued to grow, some even reaching the size of regular towns. The nearest one was also the largest, so that's where Lester began his search for Hannah. Several men, most of them in civilian clothes, were standing near the entrance to a large complex bustling with activity. Lester always felt a little more confident in approaching civilians when he was in uniform.

He walked up to an older man who seemed to be in charge and asked him, "Has there been a school set up in this camp yet?"

The man's reply was encouraging, "Third building on the left, the large one, is our school. They're only teaching reading and writing there for now, but you will be surprised when you see that some of the students are as old as you, some older."

"The desire to read and write doesn't go away with age. I saw it in friends back in Scott County. Would one of the teachers here be a very young lady, with blonde hair and slight of build?" a hopeful Lester asked.

"There's Miss Hannah," the man nodded. "The children all adore her."

"That has to be her! Is she holding class today?" he couldn't hide his excitement.

"Till three o'clock," the man volunteered as he reached for his pocket watch. "It's two forty-five now. There's a place to sit in front of the building if you decide to wait for her."

He thanked the man for his help and strode toward the large, hastily-constructed building. From the bench where he sat, Lester could hear the cheerful chorus of children with a few adult voices mixed in as they recited from their primers. The sound of so many people experiencing their freedom was heartening to Lester, who was always looking for something good to come from this war. Shortly after the recitation ended, Hannah emerged from the building, surrounded by enthusiastic youngsters.

Lester's first encounter with Hannah in more than a year was a welcome change from the all-male company in the Army. She greeted him warmly and suggested they walk to a quiet corner of the commissary where they could find a cup of coffee and share their wartime experiences. Hannah reminded him of their conversation in front of the Huntsville post office. "You must have taken my advice and escaped when you did. Nobody is safe there now."

"I often wondered how you were faring every time the Army bypassed the upper valley. I didn't like the feeling of being unable to help, so I'm especially relieved to see you safe. A relative here in Nashville told me about a young lady boarding a train in Knoxville with her servant. Was that you and Jake? Do you know where he's at now?"

Hannah said, "It was easier then. The soldiers knew my father and let us both on the train. My parents wanted me to go south all the way to Atlanta, but I had planned all along to reach Union lines. Jake wanted to enlist in the Army, but they weren't recruiting Blacks yet. I suppose he's in one of the camps, but I never saw him here. He seemed interested in Memphis for some reason, but he could never make it there with this war going on."

"Memphis? Why would he go there?" Lester looked puzzled.

"He may think he has family there. It would be hard to find anyone in Memphis now. There are four camps like this plus more nearby. The healthy men are volunteering for the Army, so the camps fill up with women, children, the infirm," was all Hannah could tell him.

"I wish I could find Jake. When everyone else in Scott County was looking out for himself, Jake helped me escape," Lester said with some emotion. "And how about your family? Still in Scott County?"

Hannah sighed, "My brother Willard fought under Zollicoffer, then was among those sent by Albert Sidney Johnston to Fort Donelson. He was one of the twelve thousand men delivered up to Grant on terms of *unconditional surrender*. He was exchanged in May, but died at Perryville in October. Were you in that battle?"

"My regiment has not fought in a real battle since I enlisted after Mill Springs," Lester hated to admit. "We sure do our share of marching, though. All over Tennessee, Kentucky, Alabama. I hope we make a serious effort to take Chattanooga now that Rosecrans is in command. Imagine a shabby railroad town becoming a major military objective. I hear tell that all the army commanders are demanding more resources than Washington can possibly supply. The Army of the Potomac is now under Joe Hooker and he has to rebuild that army after Burnside's disaster at Fredericksburg. He needs cavalry, Rosecrans needs cavalry, and there are never enough trained troopers or horses. With Grant no closer to Vicksburg, the three main armies sit idle and impatient to get it over with."

"When do you think you'll set out for Chattanooga?" Hannah asked.

Lester told her, "I can only sum up what the men in camp are saying about the situation Rosecrans faces. Nothing can move in the winter without a river or at least a reliable railroad to transport men and supplies. Lincoln, Congress, voters – they're all demanding action. Most of us never want to see mud again when this war is over. I've never been over the country between Murfreesboro and Chattanooga, but it's probably as bad as everywhere else we're been on the plateau. At least we have a secure supply line where we are, but Bragg has to bring supplies all the way up from Atlanta through Chattanooga. Rosy will get heat from Washington to move before long. 1862 didn't end well for the North and the Emancipation Proclamation is a mockery without military success to back it up. But Lincoln's armies can't provide one."

Lester still wanted to hear more about the current situation in Scott County, so he asked Hannah about her parents. Hannah told him, "Things got too hot for them. Secessionists without protection from Union partisans have no future. No matter who wins the War, the hill country will still be violent. The Confederates gave them safe passage to Chattanooga and on to Atlanta. That was shortly after Jake and I left Knoxville."

"How committed was Jake to joining the Army?" Lester asked.

"He was more determined than anything to wear that blue uniform. The Army won't free his people until they make themselves part of that army. That's how Jake explained it to me," she assured Lester.

"There must be many more like Jake who feel that way," Lester remarked. "I keep hearing stories in camp about slaves who offer to help us. They volunteer to act as scouts and give us useful information when Union forces approach. They've been sheltering escaped P.O.W.s and Confederate deserters. But I think Jake is talking about more conspicuous service, like in real combat. If Jake is successful in enlisting, I may be able to locate him through his regiment."

"He did ask whether I'd mind if he used the Clifton surname when he enlists. I was surprised he wanted any connection to my father, but it could make it easier for others to find him," reasoned Hannah. "The Army is brigading U.S.C.T. regiments here in Nashville. For now, most units are serving garrison duty all over Tennessee. Have you heard of any who have taken part in battle?"

Lester indicated disappointment, "No. Some generals doubt their ability in battle and some are reluctant to send in Black units where a high casualty count can damage a general's reputation."

Wishing he did not have to return to camp after such a pleasant afternoon, Lester announced it was time to go. His parting words were, "I have no idea where the Army will send me. Next time I see you, it could be anywhere between the Ohio River and the Gulf!"

Hannah squeezed his hand and sincerely wished him well as he departed. She had always been fond of Lester when they were growing up, and now she held him in high esteem for his service. She hoped they would meet up again, but it wouldn't be in Tennessee – or anywhere else south of the Ohio River. She had no reason to stay.

Chapter 5
War at its Worst

L ife in camp grew tedious as winter wore on. The railroad from Louisville was under constant threat as it ran though a region virtually barren of crops. Rosecrans considered Murfreesboro a critical position and set to work constructing elaborate fortifications to be held by a large garrison. The men figured Rosecrans must be feeling heat from Washington to move, while he spent more time stockpiling supplies in Murfreesboro for a move against Tullahoma.

The West Point curriculum placed emphasis on engineering, and generals liked to apply their training to the design of elaborate fortifications. The months spent in Murfreesboro produced an impregnable fortress spanning Stones River. The outer works consisted of *curtains* connecting nine *lunettes,* which are projections from the works that give artillery a wider field of fire. The inner works contained four large artillery emplacements. Rosecrans claimed the works were essential to protecting the railroad between Nashville and Chattanooga.

Mud and maneuver

On June 24, the Army of the Cumberland finally marched out of camp. Bragg's army occupied four gaps through a ridge called *Highland Rim.* Arising from a plateau called *The Barrens*, the Rim ran along the south bank of Duck River. The advance took Rosecrans's columns along narrow primitive roads that turned to mush when a downpour hit on that first day of the campaign and the next sixteen days after that. A cynical joke that spread through the ranks claimed that *Tullahoma* is formed from a combination of two Greek words: *Tulla* (mud) and *Homa* (more mud). When the joke reached the 4th Kentucky, the men asked Wilbur if he had invented it. He said he wished he had.

Rosecrans was able to out-maneuver Bragg during the advance. Partly to compensate for the deficiency in cavalry, Rosecrans had formed a brigade of mounted infantry, armed with Spencer 7-shot repeaters. Known as *Wilder's Lightning Brigade*, it was employed to great advantage in seizing two of the gaps through Highland Rim, then raiding behind Bragg's lines to sever his communications. Morale in Bragg's army continued to sink and he found it harder to stay informed or have orders obeyed. Unable to hold Tullahoma, Bragg followed the advice of his generals to retreat to Chattanooga. This is the one skill that Bragg had mastered and on July 3, the Army of Tennessee moved toward Chattanooga, after almost a year of misadventure.

Casualties on the Union side were negligible, but the army captured over sixteen hundred Rebels, many of them not so much surrendering as deserting. Lester was stunned by the appalling condition of these men. They were gaunt, some downright emaciated, many shoeless, clad in rags, dispirited. He brought up the observation in camp that night and Hubert jumped on it as another sign of hope for a short war, "If they're typical of the Confederate soldiers, we may not see another battle."

"Don't count on it," countered Grrr. "I hear Lee is raiding into Pennsylvania and Hooker can't do anything about it." The others rarely believed anything Grrr claimed to know.

Lester renewed his theory that the war would be won in the Western theater. "Grant has Vicksburg almost starved out. He and Sherman will be looking for a new fight in the West." While the men were speculating, two welcome announcements reached camp: Vicksburg's surrender to Grant and Lee's retreat from Gettysburg.

"Who defeated Lee?" asked everybody within earshot. The message was read and they learned it was George Meade. Few of them had ever heard of Meade, but they hoped he wouldn't let Lee retreat without further damage to his army.

"If that happens, the war is over before we reach the Tennessee River! If Lee gets away, we'll have to chase Bragg all the way to the Gulf," Hubert clearly indicated his preference.

Wilbur had been deep in thought, but he had little to say that could be called encouraging. He just sighed and shrugged his shoulders, "Who's going to stop this war? The Rebels keep losing territory, men, and wealth, just about everything they brought to the war. Southern Whites still do nothing to oppose Davis for fear of retaliation. Do you expect his generals to counsel surrender? They all know how it will end; it's like they're fighting not to lose what they've already lost. This madness will go on till we exhaust everything the South needs to carry on the fight."

"How long will the North support the War?" Lester wondered. "The voters were not solidly in support of continuing a war against secession to begin with. Now there's plenty of folk against a war for emancipation. All the while, casualties pile up. We had better take Chattanooga soon."

Hubert added to the gloomy outlook, as only he could do, "Well, the generals don't seem to be in a hurry to advance anywhere. Rosecrans has moved us thirty miles since January and we still have more of this lifeless plateau between us and Chattanooga. And how do we get across the river if we reach it?" Most of the regiment was growing impatient to get it over with, but less pessimistic than Hubert.

At last, on August 16, Rosecrans felt enough pressure from Washington to put his army on the march to the Tennessee River. Morale picked up as Rosecrans moved the men in multiple columns, in keeping with his preference for maneuver over battle. The terrain was much the same as what they had crossed south of Murfreesboro, largely devoid of forage and roads that were barely adequate in dry weather. Jasper remarked that he'd never seen a dry road in Tennessee.

Checkmate at Chickamauga

The infantry columns reached the river at several points below Chattanooga as well as one above. Most of the soldiers were not thrilled by their first view of what lay across the river. The city was built on a flat along the south bank, at the mouth of Chattanooga Creek. It was surrounded by a jumble of ridges, streams, gaps and mountain coves, clearings, thick woods, crude roads, and a few small farms and buildings. At first, Rosecrans benefitted from the terrain because Bragg could not guard all possible crossing points. The Union forces crossed at several places with the use of pontoons, rafts, and boats, entering the unknown in columns widely separated. Once Bragg realized Rosecrans had made it across, he had to evacuate Chattanooga to preserve his supply line coming up from Georgia. Rosecrans's generals advised consolidating his position in that city, which he would need as his base of supply. Thinking the Rebels were in headlong retreat, he gambled that an aggressive pursuit could devastate Bragg's army.

Moving an army through this terrain was much like groping through a maze, uncertain as to what was waiting at the next turn. Rosecrans was surprised when his columns encountered enemy forces and had to conclude Bragg was not retreating at all. Once this dawned on Rosecrans, he hastened to reunite his corps and protect his line of communications with his base at Chattanooga. As it turned out, Bragg was being reinforced and intended to turn and fight. Troops from Mississippi and two divisions under Longstreet from Lee's army were to give Bragg superior numbers for a change.

The urgency of Rosecrans's situation necessitated a grueling all-night march for Thomas's corps to form the northern, or left, flank of the Union line. Here Thomas could protect Rossville Gap, on the road to Chattanooga. There had already been some probing and skirmishing as battle lines were formed from arriving units. Exhausted and parched from the march, Lester was encouraged when Croxton's brigade was given time to rest and boil coffee before being sent into line. Somewhat refreshed, Lester was still wishing he could be anywhere else but in his first true battle, soon to become known to all as *Chickamauga*.

The morning light barely penetrated the tangled woods where Lester's regiment was formed. He knew there could be Rebels moving unseen through the trees in front of him. His trepidation was increased when orders rang out for the 4th Kentucky and the rest of Croxton's brigade to advance. They ran into a large Confederate force that was attempting to turn Thomas's left flank. The battle now became general. Confused fighting ensued all along Thomas's front while arriving units of both armies extended the battle line further south. Brannon's division was sent to the endangered left flank to meet the Confederate attacks. During that action, Croxton's brigade was pulled out of Brannon's line and replaced by a fresh brigade. After fighting without respite since the battle opened, Croxton's men were out of ammunition. When they rejoined Brannon, the division had been shifted to form the right end of Thomas's line. They remained in defense of that position until darkness ended the day's fighting.

Lester had endured some miserable nights before, as every infantryman must, but this was the worst. The men slept in line of battle, with fires forbidden. Many of them had dropped their knapsacks further back, along with their blankets and coats. From the gloomy woods in front came the sounds of wounded men who could not be reached safely in the deadly no-man's land. As the men coped with the conditions brought on by the freezing night, Jasper asked those near him, "What do you think is worse – trying to survive this night or wondering what the dawn will bring along with warmer temperatures? All I hear from the Rebel lines are sounds of enemy units moving back and forth."

"I sometimes think I hear train whistles not far from here," added Hubert. "What direction are we facing?"

Wilbur told him, "We are facing east, with the rest of Thomas's line on our left. The troops coming in on our right are from Thomas Crittenden's corps, but if you'd heard the things I did today, you'd know Rosecrans is mixing up all the divisions without regard to corps organization."

"Where will Bragg hit us in the morning?" Hubert hoped it would not be on the 4th Kentucky's front.

"Today they were trying to flank our left. That's why the action was so hot when we ran out of ammunition. If he's being reinforced, he can throw in more brigades anywhere he wants. Most of Thomas's command will be piling up breastworks in the morning," Wilbur muttered.

Most men managed a few fitful hours of sleep before the morning sun brought a bit of welcome warmth along with dread over the impending Confederate attack. All along the line, Thomas's divisions were taking advantage of the delay in Bragg's attack to improve the breastworks with timber, fence rails, rocks, and earth in that sector.

Thus fortified, the five divisions under Thomas repulsed several disjointed Rebel attacks over the course of the day.

Meanwhile, to the right of Brannon, everything was about to degenerate into chaos. While Union brigades were still coming into line, the men in the 4th Kentucky could tell from distant sounds and glimpses through the trees that a heavy attack column was massing opposite the Union center. The night before, Longstreet had arrived with two more brigades from his Virginia command in time for this, the second day of battle, in addition to the three that had fought on Day 1. Longstreet's last three brigades and his artillery were too late for this battle.

Lester felt some degree of relief when he saw reinforcements coming up behind Brannon's division. Then to the horror of everyone in line who was close enough to see, these turned out to be two brigades pulling out of line from Brannon's right! Rosecrans had lost track of the position of his units and in his confusion created a half-mile gap and now Longstreet's attack was made directly into this part of the Union line. The Union center and right were thrown back in confusion and units disintegrated into scattered fragments. Croxton was badly wounded in the action and succeeded by William Hayes in brigade command. Lester recalled later how leaderless men were milling around the field looking for someone to give them orders. Much of the brigade fled through McFarland's Gap in Missionary Ridge to their rear as they were joined by Rosecrans and two corps commanders in flight to Chattanooga. Casualties were high in the 4th KY which, added to the many who were swept up in the panicked retreat and some who fell in with other fragments of units, left only forty-five men to stay and fight on as part of the brigade.

The terrain directly behind the ruptured line of battle in this sector featured a long, irregular ridge that ended at slightly higher *Snodgrass Hill* on its east end. Brannon and other officers began forming stragglers along the crest of what came to be called *Horseshoe Ridge*. Thomas was now ranking officer on the field and after throwing back one more attack on his left, he consolidated his troops and moved his headquarters behind this determined line. When the men saw him personally directing the battle, it served as a much-needed boost to their morale. Thomas had chosen a position favorable to defense and repulsed repeated attacks, most of them uncoordinated, until he was nearly out of ammunition. Just then, two brigades from the small reserve corps of Gordon Granger arrived from Rossville Gap, where they had been protecting the line of retreat. They brought with them a new supply of ammunition that enabled Thomas's men to hold the line until darkness, when he was able to conduct an orderly withdrawal to Rossville. The men were fully drained of energy but able to rejoin the rest of the army in Chattanooga the next day.

A mixture of disbelief, exhaustion, and despondency pervaded all the units that regrouped in Chattanooga. The soldiers knew that someone had committed a tragic mistake that led to the disaster on the second day. Recriminations were mumbled among the men. Officers were more audible in theirs, especially those directed toward the high command who had abandoned them on the field. The only reputation that survived the battle was that of George Thomas, who will be forever known to history as *The Rock of Chickamauga*.

When the fractured regiments were reassembled in the Chattanooga camp, the muster roll for the 4th Kentucky showed 160 men and 13 officers as killed and wounded. The regiment had gone into battle with 360 and 19, respectively. Every man in the regiment had experienced the hell of one of the War's most desperate and savage battles. Only Gettysburg, three months earlier, exceeded Chickamauga in casualty count. Lester's comrades were completely spent and for some it took several days for the shock of battle to wear off. Lester had lost some good friends – all the men had – and the sorrow was deepened by the idea of being humiliated by the Rebels. The survivors in the 4th Kentucky had been scattered in the rupture of the Union center. Nobody could be faulted for being swept up in a stampede to the rear. Most of those who had stayed to fight and survived on Snodgrass Hill rarely mentioned the experience to the others.

An army under siege

Morale declined further when it became known that Rosecrans had abandoned the heights around Chattanooga to Bragg, who promptly fortified Missionary Ridge and Lookout Mountain. To the troops in the city below, this meant they were under siege. The guns atop Lookout commanded the river, the railroad, and the wagon road that ran through the valley. Only a small fraction of what the army needed could be supplied over the crude, barely usable roads across the rugged plateau they had recently crossed. Except for that sixty-mile mud-pit, there was no way in and no way out. The men soon felt the effects of siege as rations were cut, animals starved, and the army was ill-prepared for the approaching winter.

In this small city, anything that could be co-opted for military use was soon consumed, including trees that had once grown in the area. Residents who had decided to stay – and there were Unionists in town – watched as buildings were torn down for their lumber, though soldiers accorded people some measure of respect. Rosecrans tried to cheer the troops with personal visits to various units, but nothing of substance was being done to improve the deteriorating situation. The men didn't hear it till later, but back in Washington, the President was describing Rosecrans as "acting confused and stunned, like a duck hit on the head."

An army under siege must maintain a sort of courage different from what is demanded in battle, which can be horribly unnerving but usually of short duration, with a well-defined beginning and end. Here in Chattanooga, the men languished with a gnawing sense of inability to prevent their eventual fate.

"Rosecrans led us into a trap!" Hubert whimpered. "We wanted this city so we could move south to Atlanta. Now we can't go in any direction. We're doomed here!"

"Be reasonable," snapped Wilbur. "Do you think Lincoln will just accept losing the Army of the Cumberland as a cost of war and concede next year's election? We have U.S. forces positioned all along the western rivers who can find a way in. Lincoln has to hold Chattanooga. He'll use every resource he has."

Lester added, "Lincoln still can't do anything for my old neighbors under Rebel occupation."

One of the men from the area east of Bowling Green had some encouraging information for Lester, "Some of the prisoners we took on the first day of battle were from Simon Buckner's corps. He had been headquartered in Knoxville till he was ordered to reinforce Bragg. He left only two thousand men to guard Cumberland Gap and the upper valley. I don't know who replaced Buckner."

"I know!" blurted an exultant Grrr. "Lincoln sent Ambrose Burnside to march from Lexington to Knoxville. He crossed the ridges west of the Gap and fit his way into Knoxville in early September. I heard it from a sergeant who read it in the Nashville paper before he rejoined his unit."

"Burnside?" chimed in everyone within earshot. "The author of the Fredericksburg fiasco?"

"Makes sense," said Wilbur. "That's the way the Army works. They send the disappointments west and we lose the good ones to the East. Remember Pope after Second Bull Run? He's in Minnesota now."

"So who comes here? Hooker?" Hubert muttered sarcastically. "And where do they send Rosecrans? Nevada?"

Help is on the way

Just then, one of Captain Latrobe's company staff officers walked up with the news that a powerful effort was underway to rescue the Army of the

Cumberland and establish firm control of the entire Tennessee Valley. "Meade is sending 23,000 infantry from Virginia under Joe Hooker by rail to Stevenson, Alabama, just a few miles downriver. Grant is also sending 20,000 under Sherman."

"How long will that take?" an unimpressed Grrr snarled. "Hooker must have a thousand miles to cover."

"Twelve hundred," said the clerk. "The Army has an arrangement with the railroads and telegraph that makes operations like this possible. What I don't know is how they reach us in this hole once they're off the train."

After a few more days of meager rations, the men noticed an increase in activity around army headquarters. Some reported that they saw General Rosecrans with his chief-of-staff James A. Garfield as they mounted up and rode north along the tortuous supply route. Word soon reached the men that General Thomas had received a telegram ordering him to assume command of the besieged army. The order came from Grant, who had just been elevated to command of the entire theater of war that lay between the Appalachians and the Trans-Mississippi. Grant was on his way personally to Chattanooga to conduct operations. Most of the men preferred to serve under Thomas, but Wilbur reasoned that generals as diverse in temperament as Sherman, Hooker, and Thomas needed Lincoln's favorite general in overall charge.

On October 23, not long after this exchange, Wilbur and Lester strolled toward Thomas's headquarters and asked men standing around if they had seen more generals than usual. An older volunteer started in cynically, "We were here most of the time waiting to see what was going on. A bunch of officers rode up during the evening. The shortest one had to be helped off his horse and limped into the building. He was the only officer with two stars, so we supposed that had to be Grant."

Another offered, "Grant probably fell off his horse again. It's a good thing the Army of the Cumberland will still be under Thomas if we ever get out of this hole. I heard that Rosecrans is being transferred to Missouri, in keeping with Army practice."

Good news often travels more slowly in war, maybe because it doesn't require immediate reaction. It was just now being reported that Grant had met briefly with Rosecrans before his agonizing two-day ride into Chattanooga. He also met with Hooker, whose troops had begun arriving only four days after departing Virginia. The full complement of 23,000 was at Stevenson by 11 ½ days, along with their artillery, wagons, horses, and baggage. The men were growing more impressed with the vast advantage that the North enjoyed in production and infrastructure. Jasper remarked, "Look how the South has to move on rickety railroads. While we have the *Military Railroad* and *Military Telegraph*. It won't be long before we have the *Military-Industrial Complex!*"

A new energy seemed to be infused in camp after the change in command. Only three days since Grant's arrival, Wm. Hazen's brigade from Thomas's infantry, under the cover of darkness, floated pontoon boats down the Tennessee to surprise and overpower Confederate pickets on the south bank at Brown's Ferry, just down-river from Lookout Mountain. More men materialized on the north bank with bridging materials, while the lead division of Hooker's force arrived from downriver to secure the crossing. Grant now had a direct supply line up the valley that men dubbed the *Cracker Line*. Within days, they were back on full rations and speculating on what was next to come. When Sherman's divisions came up from Vicksburg on November 21, they went into camp upstream on the north bank, across from the northern end of Missionary Ridge.

Hooker was camped at the mouth of Lookout Creek, which flows along the western base of the long ridge that ends in the steep peak of Lookout Mountain. Bragg ordered Longstreet to dislodge Hooker from the valley but only a feeble effort was made with predictable failure. Morale had sunk so low among Bragg's generals they became mutinous. Jefferson Davis made a personal visit to Bragg's headquarters in hopes of easing the situation. Part of his solution involved sending Longstreet with his divisions upriver to reoccupy Knoxville. The move further thinned the ranks that were besieging Chattanooga, especially those around Lookout Mountain.

In camp, Lester and his comrades were sorting through the succession of changes in command. "I hear Brannon has been transferred to the artillery so we're getting a new division commander," were Wilbur's first words when he returned from another information-gathering stroll. "We'll be in Absalom Baird's division – our whole brigade."

"Is Colonel Croxton recovered from Chickamauga?" Hubert asked.

"A colonel named Edward Phelps will command the

brigade while Croxton heals. Since General Thomas was promoted to army command, our new corps commander is John Palmer," Wilbur summarized. "Alexander McCook and Thomas Crittenden have been removed from corps command after they fled the field at Chickamauga. Their commands have been consolidated into one corps, under Gordon Granger. The 4th Kentucky has a new commander – a former staff officer named William Kelly."

"When are we going to fight our way out of here?" everybody wanted to know. The tedium and confinement under siege were growing more unbearable by the day. They were not aware of the pressure being exerted on Grant to begin the breakout. Most men in the ranks were intent on avenging their humiliation, it was clear, but Mr. Lincoln was even more anxious over the condition of Burnside in Knoxville, as Longstreet was threatening the city.

Grant had been going to great exertion in organizing these disparate forces that had come from three different armies. He wanted to mount the offensive as soon as he could, especially since he had to secure Chattanooga before he could send aid to Burnside. Lester tried injecting a positive thought, "Try to imagine what must be going through Bragg's mind when he knows he's about to be struck by Grant, Thomas, Sherman, Hooker. The pickets are saying that Bragg's men are no better off than we were before the Cracker Line. No doubt we'll bring in a whole new draft of deserters and prisoners."

The breakout

On November 23, only a month after Grant arrived, he was ready to mount an offensive against Bragg's lines, high above Chattanooga. The first movement was made by Thomas, who advanced his army in a grand display of parade-ground marching to Orchard Knob, half the distance to Missionary Ridge. The knob served as battle headquarters for the duration of the assault. That same day, Hooker advanced with two divisions on Lookout Mountain by starting on the western slope and then traversing the northern tip, slowly gaining elevation. By the time they encountered the surprised Rebels on the eastern slope, the cloud cover obscured the action from the rest of the army below. The men could hear the firing shift and lose intensity, then cease, but it was not until morning when a gust of wind blew the clouds from the summit and revealed the U.S. flag flying triumphantly and declaring victory in the *Battle Above the Clouds*. Now it was expected that Hooker would continue to the south end of Missionary Ridge while Sherman attacked the northern end. Thomas's four divisions stood in reserve, facing the center of Bragg's line. From left to right were the divisions of Baird, Wood, Sheridan, and Johnson. The 4th Kentucky, with the rest of Phelps's brigade, represented the left of Baird's line. Thomas's men knew that Grant had assigned them a secondary role because he doubted their fighting strength after Chickamauga.

The battle that had opened so skillfully soon encountered major obstacles. For Hooker, it was swollen Chattanooga Creek, which runs between

Lookout and Missionary Ridge. The Rebels had burned the bridge when they retreated from Lookout, delaying Hooker for four hours. At the north end, Sherman discovered he had been relying on a faulty map, which led him to a peak separated from the true ridge by a narrow ravine. Despite his overwhelming numbers, he could make no headway. Lester could almost feel every man in the regiment grip his musket firmly in anticipation of important orders. This was different from previous battles when they wished they could be anywhere else. They had twice chased this Confederate army across Kentucky and Tennessee; now it was time to settle the issue. Even Thomas, much less Grant, did not sense the intensity of the desire to exact revenge continuing to build within the Army of the Cumberland when at last the signal to advance belched from six cannons on Orchard Knob. As 25,000 men stepped off, Lester looked to his right, awed by the magnificence of this perfectly-aligned front, drums pounding, every man wearing a look of determination as they closed in on the Rebel rifle-pits at the base of the ridge. It was Grant's intent that they halt after evicting this thin line at the base; this was to be only a demonstration to draw pressure from Sherman's front. To the Rebels, it appeared that Thomas's men had no plans to stop. Some fired one shot before retreating up the ridge, others fled without firing, and a resolute few remained in the pits, only to be captured.

Not all attacking units reached the rifle pits at the same moment and once they did, it seemed every officer had a different understanding of Grant's orders. Some tried to halt their men at the base, while others urged them up the slope. The irregular topography of the slope factored in too. In some parts of the line, the men were sheltered from the plunging artillery fire from the crest, while others found themselves under a hail of shot and shell. The 4th Kentucky hesitated only briefly since others in line were already pursuing the fleeing Rebel skirmishers up the slope. Units lost all formation as the ragged line encountered boulders, ravines, vines, bushes, and some open ground. Bragg's guns were positioned on the topographical crest, where the muzzles could not be depressed enough to fire on advancing Yankees.

Fifty-five minutes after they had stepped off in well-ordered ranks, Thomas's men were swarming over the Rebel guns at the crest, taking delight in the stampede of Bragg's army back to Georgia. The spontaneous celebration at the top could be heard for miles. The exultation shared by the men of the 4th Kentucky was intensified by the feeling of redemption for men caught up in the flight on the second day at Chickamauga. Now every man on the field was wishing that General Thomas could identify him individually as he aggressively charged the Confederate works.

The terrain allowed for Bragg to maintain a rear-guard action that discouraged a prolonged pursuit, and Grant recalled the men back to their camps. Casualties were not as high as in other battles, but Colonel Phelps, who had served in Croxton's absence, was mortally wounded in the charge. Brigade command again devolved to Colonel William Hays.

Lester was still reluctant to revel in lifting the siege until the Rebels under Longstreet were driven out of the upper valley. Fully aware of the urgency, Grant assigned Granger to the task. As Granger dragged his feet, Grant sent Sherman, who always carried out assignments promptly. Burnside had been surprisingly effective in protecting Knoxville from Longstreet and now with Sherman approaching, Longstreet thought it prudent to retreat closer to the mountains in Virginia, where he wintered before rejoining Lee for the spring campaign. The news that the upper valley would be occupied by a Union force for the duration of the war ended Lester's two years of fretting over the safety of his mother in Knoxville.

Chattanooga, U.S.A.

With Tennessee largely cleared of enemy troops, the Army of the Cumberland went into winter camp at Chattanooga. The city's military importance was enormous, justifying the long and costly efforts to secure it. Otherwise the town had little to recommend it. Before the war, the small population of Chattanooga had benefitted from its location as a transportation hub. Now it was at the center of military operations in the Western theater. The army quickly repaired railroads in all directions and procured additional rolling stock.

Chattanooga was more fortunate than some towns visited by the armies during the first two years of war. The towns garrisoned by Federal troops stood a better chance of surviving, though they would never be the same. Since the Proclamation went into effect, the influx of slaves seeking freedom led to the creation of more refugee camps near permanently-occupied towns. Chattanooga received six thousand fugitives of all ages arriving from Georgia. A new camp had to be established to accommodate them, so land on the north side of the river was provided. The Army called it *Camp Contraband*, for lack of originality. It was a more humane location than some that had been established earlier. The newly-emancipated were provided opportunities for paid employment and permission to form a self-governing body for the camp. Still, neglect, disease, and overwork were all too often experienced.

As the camp was filling up with freed people, Lester decided to cross the river and perhaps find a familiar face from Scott County. He didn't expect to find Jake, who had made it to Nashville a year ago. Most of the new arrivals had come from Northern Georgia and Alabama. More refugees were coming in as intact families now that less risk was involved in reaching friendly lines. The Army had established the camp on the north side of the river with the official explanation that the site would be less exposed to Rebel artillery fire. Something about this didn't make sense to Lester, but he continued to the camp where everybody seemed busy turning it into a home. While surveying the scene from where he stood, Lester noticed an elderly couple being made comfortable by younger refugees. It seemed that everyone had a job to do and needed no military supervision. When Lester approached the man and woman, he introduced himself and learned their names were James and Hattie.

"When did you reach the camp?" he opened the conversation.

James sounded weary, but clearly pleased to be safe under the protection of the Army. "We spent most of our life in Monroe County, up the valley from here. We been watchin' Rebels, then Lincoln men go back and forth through there between August and the end of the fightin' down here. We couldn't leave till then. Only been here two days."

"I think that will keep Rebels out of the valley for good. I got family up in Knoxville," Lester smiled broadly, knowing his own people were safe.

Hattie nodded and said, "Our two boys said it was time to try to get here, so they loaded a farm wagon and hitched up the mules. Me and James rode in the bed and the boys handled the team. Took us four days to get here, but we're safe now."

"Where's your sons?" Lester asked them.

"They wanted to join the Army, but they had to go all the way to the big camp in Corinth to do it," James said with visible pride.

After a few more minutes of watching the settlement take shape, Lester slowly made his way back to his unit. The old man and woman had deeply affected him. Freedom was so precious they did not seem to mind the discomforts and crude accommodations in a contraband camp now that they could live free for their remaining years.

As predicted, Chattanooga received a number of White refugees who were destitute, along with a sizeable number of deserters from the Confederate Army who brought with them sad tales of life deeper in the South. All the regiment had seen of the South so far were parts near the Union frontier. The damage and chaos caused by the armies was not surprising, but many soldiers thought that further back from the lines, the South was unaffected, that plantation life remained untroubled by the fighting still hundreds of miles away. Now they were hearing accounts from several Confederate deserters in camp that gave them a new look at what was happening on the heart of Dixie.

A group of half-starved Rebels had decided that an uncertain future with the Yankees was preferable to remaining in the Southern army. While the Rebels were wolfing down the rations offered to them, they gave an alarming account of the home-front. A young private named Marvin, from Mississippi, spoke first, "I didn't have no slaves and didn't want to fight for them that did. I was barely making it working hard on my little farm with my wife and children helping. All we could raise was enough food for us to live on. I don't know what my family will do now that I'm far away and the countryside is so dangerous. My regiment has been in Bragg's army since the retreat to Tupelo in May of 1862."

Marvin appeared sickly and malnourished. To him, Union rations were a rare feast. "In our army, corn meal and rancid pork are the usual fare – if we get any rations at all. No vegetables but plenty of weevils Men lose their teeth. A third of us are without shoes. By the time our pay comes, the dollar ain't worth shucks. We can't spend it anyhow when sellers only take gold or Yankee greenbacks."

Jerome was a man in his thirties from the interior of Georgia, some distance south of Atlanta in cotton country. He had a family he had been hoping to see once the army retreated south from Kentucky in October of 1862. Some soldiers were given leave to go home long enough to bring in the harvest, then return to the ranks. Others went without leave but returned before being considered deserters. From them, and from the distressing letters from home their fellow soldiers were receiving, Jerome learned that even in areas untouched by the armies, the war was visiting hardships on the civilians. Tales of hunger, despair, and impoverishment ran through the Rebel army. "The Davis government is waging this senseless war on the backs of the poor. Impressment agents take all the food people count on for the winter. They run off with horses and mules, salt for preserving meat. All the while, the planters keep growing cotton even though Davis tells them to grow food. Crops go unattended when slaves refuse to work or run off. Women and children ain't safe when most men of military age are in the army. They're drafting boys of seventeen now. The countryside is too dangerous for women and children, so families move into towns where there is work in war production. And the towns then swell with starving people where there is no food but plenty of anger. There are food riots in cities where desperate women with children to feed break into stores. You folks up north got no idea what we're going through in Georgia in a war that has no end."

Chapter 6
A Welcome Interlude

The men in camp later discussed what they were learning about the extent of the hardships that were falling on the Southerners and disruptions so far from the actual fighting. Wilbur mused, "I wonder what we'll find when we reach Atlanta. I was picturing an elegant, thriving community that outclasses Boston or Philadelphia, but after listening to that Jerome fellow, I imagine the citizens of Atlanta are feeling much dread now that we're only one hundred miles away."

Hubert hoped he wouldn't have to fight in another battle. For him, the shock of Chickamauga hadn't worn off. "We won't have to go to Atlanta. When the spring campaign opens, Lincoln will throw everything he has against Richmond. Defeat Lee and the war is over by election time."

"Defeat Lee? Who? McClellan? Pope? Burnside? Hooker? Meade? The President doesn't need more men. He needs a general," Wilbur said with some conviction.

Grrr chimed in, "I hear Lincoln might send General Thomas."

The rumor disturbed Lester, whose admiration for Thomas had been a source of optimism during the most troubling times. "Then he'll send us one of his paper-collar Easterners. I'd hate to lose Old Pap. He's the only reason this army is still together."

Wilbur assured him, "Thomas won't go. Lincoln won't send him. He has too many connections to Virginia. He was Lee's closest associate in the Old Army for ten years. If he went back to Virginia, nobody would trust him. I think he's where he wants to be."

The 4th Kentucky spent Christmas in the Chattanooga camp. It made for dreary holiday, the third for most of the men. Their enlistment periods were expiring and the prospect of returning home with an honorable discharge was appealing. It had been two years since Mill Springs, when Lester first joined the regiment. He had been in only two pitched battles while others in Croxton's brigade had fought in as many as six. Now Lester was torn between his original plan to go somewhere far from the war and the reluctance to abandon his comrades in the field. Now in January of 1864, he was watching the massive buildup of war materials for the anticipated drive on Atlanta come spring. The prospect of being part of this powerful host of 110,000 men began to appeal to him and many of his fellow soldiers. The Confederacy was growing weaker every day and the majority of men Lester knew in camp wanted to see the task through to the end. The officers were trying hard to stress the importance of maintaining army strength as the best way to promote reenlistment.

One afternoon, Captain Latrobe came by on a casual visit to the camp of Lester's mess-mates. Lately he seemed unusually appreciative of the men in his company. He spent some time every day sitting down for a friendly chat to encourage reenlistment. Vane Latrobe was a lawyer in Covington Kentucky, across the Ohio River from Cincinnati, where he raised an infantry company at his own expense and the men elected him to be their captain. With little military experience at first, he displayed a natural talent for leadership. He considered it important to keep the men informed on the progress of the war. A small knot of soldiers gathered around him as he reported how things stood. "Lately, we've been winning this war on the battlefield and by every other measure. There is no way the South can ever hope to score a military victory with what they have left to fight with. We're just not winning fast enough. At last, it's come down to a war of wills to see who blinks first. That will be us if we don't have this war won by the November elections. Davis knows all the South has to do is keep its armies in the field to prevent us from making significant military gains. While this is going on, the civilians suffer more every day for a cause they dare not criticize or question. To the Confederates, 1863 was a disastrous year. Stonewall Jackson was killed at Chancellorsville and Lee nearly wrecked his army at Gettysburg. Losing Vicksburg meant no more horses, cattle, pork, salt, and chemicals for gunpowder from the Trans-Mississippi. My lord, I'm told there are towns where a wagon is sent out every morning to collect urine from chamber-pots to extract niter for saltpeter."

Unable to resist the set-up, Jasper chimed in, "And it's piss-poor gunpowder they make with it! I never saw any of their shells land or explode where they're supposed to. Good thing for us!"

The amused captain continued, "It doesn't stop there. The naval blockade keeps tightening and the

South can't produce what it used to import. When we took Chattanooga, we cut off access to the Ducktown mine, which accounted for 90% of the South's copper supply. They're melting down copper stills at a time when whiskey is the only way some hill folks can make it through the war. Soldiers go without shoes for lack of leather or salt to cure it. Much of the cavalry is riding on worn-out nags barely fit for transportation to the fighting. You're seeing tons of war materials building up here. Do you think it's that way in Richmond or Atlanta? In areas where food can be grown far from the reach of troops or impressments agents, it rots in a warehouse or on a platform because the transportation system is so decrepit. Iron rails wear out and replacing them means scavenging other lines. Davis is widely unpopular. He's lost the support of governors and citizens, but they let him carry on this war."

The captain summed up the political reality, "The voters won't be satisfied even with the progress we're making in what has become a war of attrition. When the spring campaigns begin, our armies will have to engage in heavier fighting than we've seen so far."

Time away from war

The men of the 4th Kentucky would have some time to prepare themselves for the hard campaigning ahead, since the Army was offering a thirty-day veterans' furlough and a $400 bounty to those who volunteered to reenlist. An added inducement was the prospect of their regiment's conversion to the 4th Kentucky *Mounted* Infantry. Lester pictured himself on a horse with pleasure, after two years of marching for hundreds of miles over miserable roads and terrain. Predictably, Wilbur spoke of little else for days.

There were other reasons Lester decided to reenlist. It had become obvious that Scott County and its neighbors would never be at peace until the rest of the Confederacy was suppressed. His family was now the 4th Kentucky and he wanted to be with them while they went on fighting. The men were leaving camp on furlough proud of their service in a war that had already lasted longer and reached more shocking levels of devastation and human tragedy than could have been imagined when they enthusiastically volunteered in 1861.

"If I can spend a month some place where I can forget about what I've seen these past two years, I should be in good fighting spirit when I rejoin the ranks," Lester tried to tell himself.

Most of the men had families and friends in Kentucky, but Lester had to face the fact that he had no safe place to call home. For now, the area surrounding Louisville seemed as good a place as any. He had saved much of his army pay and reenlistment bounty, so he looked forward to the comforts of the city.

As goods and resources flowed into Chattanooga, they strained the capacity of the rail system. Northbound trains had more space, so the men on furlough were able to leave camp without delay. Those in the regiment who were not reenlisting remained in camp until their term of enlistment expired. Lester had not slept in a real bed since leaving home, so he decided to spend a night in

Nashville before continuing north. The slow travel and harsh winter weather reinforced his decision, as he arrived in Nashville late that night, cold and weary. He registered for a room in the first hotel he came to and fell asleep as soon as he stretched out on the soft bed. He couldn't remember the last time he'd slept so peacefully. There were no muskets or cannons firing, no officers barking orders, no wet ground to sleep on, and no enemy nearby. When Lester woke up in Nashville, he felt somewhat rejuvenated, but then he looked out his window. Daylight revealed that while the Rebels were gone from Tennessee, Nashville was a city still actively at war. Without delay, he completed his trip to Louisville.

The train between Nashville and Louisville ran through a countryside that the 4th Kentucky had marched through three times before and each time it looked more desolate. It showed the signs of armies marching, fighting, foraging, and fortifying. When the soldiers weren't there, the guerrillas and outlaws ranged through the central part of Kentucky and Tennessee. Fields had lain fallow, fence rails had gone to firewood, livestock was run off, food was scarce, and slaves had left to enlist in the U.S. Army.

Passing through this dismal land did nothing to cheer the war-weary soldier, so Lester tried not to let the sight affect him. Two years of war had hardened Lester, as it had done with many other soldiers. It was the only way he thought he could keep functioning through the course of war – to learn how not to feel. The acres of carnage left on the Shiloh battlefield began a numbing process that sustained him from that point on through the charge up Missionary Ridge. He could continue to care about the lives of his comrades who depended on each other, but when he aimed his musket in combat, he remained detached from the result of the shot.

No peace in Louisville

Lester was disappointed in the surroundings the moment he stepped off the train. Louisville was not the place to take his mind off the war for a month. It was as much a military base as Nashville and Chattanooga. Tons of food and military supplies were regularly unloaded on the Ohio River docks for shipment to the armies farther south. Thousands of U.S. soldiers could be found in Louisville at any one time, many on their way to the front or returning home either wounded or having served their enlistment terms. Other soldiers were stationed to garrison the elaborate fortifications. Confederate P.O.W.'s, Union deserters, and political prisoners were housed in a new military prison complex that occupied an entire city block. Hospitals to treat wounded men were erected by the War Department and the U.S. Sanitary Commission.

With so many soldiers in town, entrepreneurs flocked in to offer photographic portraits to send home, gambling, military goods, liquor, and brothels. A large contraband camp was set up to provide quarters, a church, and a school to teach reading to children and adults. Slavery was dying out in Kentucky, even though the state was not subject to the Proclamation. Louisville was still beset by conflict between guerrillas and Union soldiers.

Harsher measures brought more resistance. Lester visited only one saloon during his stay and that one time was unexpectedly brief. He strode up to the bar and ordered a shot of whiskey. After a minute or so, two local warf rats stumbled in and sat at a table before they noticed Lester. The mirror behind the bar clearly reflected the hostile intent triggered by his blue uniform. Without showing any alarm, Lester sipped the rest of his drink and set the empty glass on the bar. He casually turned toward he saloon doors, clutched the imagined injury under his left pant-leg, and limped out of the joint in a most convincing display of disability. Once outside, he rounded a corner, his wound magically healed, and sprinted toward the U.S. soldiers who were guarding the waterfront.

"Private McGill, 4th Kentucky!" were Lester's first words. "I was running to stay ahead of two toughs who saw me in the saloon around the corner!" he added, still out of breath.

"Where is the 4th Kentucky serving?" asked a soldier who looked to be barely eighteen.

"We were in camp at Chattanooga where they gave us a thirty-day furlough. Where are you men from?"

"Cincinnati!" the other, possibly older man responded. "Our regiment was just formed and this is our first duty south of the Ohio. I think we're being sent to Chattanooga. Did you fight there?"

When Lester nodded, they bombarded him with questions. Lester abruptly stopped talking for a moment as he searched for a way to deflect questions that called for unpleasant detail. These men were probably already filled with apprehension. Lester was hoping to spend his furlough where he was not constantly reminded of Bloody Pond at Shiloh, the disaster at Chickamauga, mud marches that went beyond the limits of endurance, or once-healthy soldiers sent to an asylum with a condition that science had yet to name.

Lester changed the subject to, "What's it like in Cincinnati?"

"It's a city where most people are actively Lincolnites. There's all kinds of war production on the river. The civilians support the soldiers any way they can. Got me to decide on joining up. Is that why you reenlisted?"

"Partly. That and a sense of loyalty to my friends in the regiment," Lester acknowledged his recent thinking.

One positive aspect of serving in the Army was the camaraderie among all who wore the blue, no matter the situation. Men came from all over the country, even a few from Southern states, to fight for the Union as they envisioned it. Background and status mean nothing when you're in battle. Lester had been away from his regiment only a few days and was already missing the esprit de corps. That saloon incident would have been less threatening if he were drinking with Grrr next to him at the bar. Jasper would be cheering him up with his own unique humor in this depressing city. He was already looking forward to rejoining his comrades in camp when they would rendezvous at Fort Nelson, just south of Lexington, and spend two months there in advance of the spring campaigns. Lester wanted to go into camp feeling that his furlough was well-spent.

Cincinnati: port in storm

"Where can I go to forget about the fighting? Where is the blue uniform still respected?" Lester wondered as he peered across the Ohio River. "Is it more peaceful in Ohio?"

The recruits at the waterfront had made Cincinnati sound like a city full of people who supported the Union war effort.

"Strange," he mused, "that only a river separates two different societies. Grant, Sherman, and Sheridan – they were all from Ohio." He didn't know what he'd do once he arrived, but said decisively, "Cincinnati has to be the place."

He slung his knapsack and found a transport carrying men who had just mustered out. They could look forward to a warm welcome on their return home. In the South, a man came home either as a casualty or a deserter.

Once on board, Lester met a group of discharged veterans who were neighbors in Cincinnati. They had enlisted together, and had served honorably. When they returned home, it was not the case of a lonely soldier coming back to an unfamiliar world. Lester had once been welcomed by a Kentucky regiment and now he was being accepted by an Ohio unit as one of their own. A man from a Rebel state with two years in the Union Army was at once a celebrity to all on board. By the time they docked in Cincinnati, Lester had been invited by about five soldiers to come home with them as their guest. He began telling his Ohio hosts that he wanted to move north once the war ended. After three weeks in Cincinnati, he would actually mean it.

The men came from homes that were among the two dozen or more houses clustered around a crossing where a neighborhood tavern was a fixture. In a city containing a large German-American population, Lester would never be far from beer or various delicacies ending in ...*wurst*. He met so many people it was impossible to remember half the names, but he would never forget Gretchen, the older sister of his new friend and host, Franz Gerlach.

The Gerlach home was an imposing three-story structure with more rooms than Lester had ever seen outside a hotel. The father, Ernst, was a congenial man most times, but an outspoken abolitionist whenever the subject arose and sometimes he didn't even need provocation. Loyalty and high competence helped him negotiate military contacts to supply iron products like rifled artillery and plating for gunboats.

The first days Lester spent in Cincinnati offered visits with families of his friends, evenings in the tavern, and freedom to wander the city, taking in all that was new to him. Lester was discovering things about himself at the same time. In the Army, a soldier is never alone. Now he was enjoying the chance to go off on his own once in a while. He was thinking less about Scott County these days. It had been a year since he last saw Hannah and by now she should be somewhere far to the North. He was taking a real liking to Cincinnati and he'd need very little encouragement to return here after the war.

One morning as Lester was setting out on one of his long walks around town, he was intercepted by Gretchen, who failed badly in making the encounter look accidental. "Lester! Where are you off to today?"

He enjoyed the sudden attention and smiled, "Today I think I'll walk along the river further downstream than I've been before. It's the first sunny day we've had since Saturday."

"Why don't you let me show you some places you might find interesting?" Gretchen volunteered.

Lester happily accepted her company and the guided walks continued on nearly a daily basis. He found Gretchen to be enjoyable company and quite intelligent, as far as his 6th -grade education allowed him to judge. She was a few years older than Lester in an era when it was becoming hard to find single men with no missing parts.

On one of their walks, they came upon a field where some school-boys were enjoying an unusually warm day with a game of baseball. "I've seen men in camp play this game before, but I didn't know children could play. I never saw it when I was in Scott County," Lester noted. "I should take one or two store-bought balls back to camp with me. Soldiers have to make their own from scraps of leather, tape, string, anything they can find. "Once I saw a ball hit so hard it exploded all over the playing field."

"What do you use for a bat?" Gretchen wondered. "Isn't that what they call it?"

"And the boy swinging at the ball is called the *batter*. There don't seem to be many rules in the game. When the soldiers play, they can whittle down a tree branch or scrap of lumber so the batter can grip it. It's good practice for swinging an empty musket when you're fightin' in the trenches."

Gretchen was clearly alarmed, "Do you ever have to fight that way?"

Lester immediately reassured her, "I won't be in the infantry ranks anymore. My regiment will be mounted now, acting a lot like cavalry but better-armed."

The time in Cincinnati was all too brief for Lester. He was immensely enjoying the time with Gretchen, but his youthful inexperience kept him from knowing what to do next.

Later toward the end of Lester's furlough, Gretchen asked him, "Where do you plan to go when this war is over? You don't talk much about Tennessee."

"I listen to my messmates every night in the 4th Kentucky camp as they recall their peaceful homes. I guess if I'm in a Kentucky regiment, my official home is Kentucky for the rest of the war," he sighed.

"That's no way to choose a home!" Gretchen sounded serious. "Why don't you picture Cincinnati as your home for the rest of the war? You've made friends here, my whole family is fond of you, and it's a peaceful city in a loyal state."

The idea immediately appealed to him and it was hard to exercise self-control lest he appear too anxious. "It would sure make me feel less like an orphan when the others talk fondly of home, especially during mail call when I'm the only one without a letter. A letter from you would cheer me up a heap."

"I'd love to correspond with you while you're in the field. What will be your mailing address?" she sounded encouraging. "And where is your civilian mail being sent?"

"Right now, my address will be Camp Nelson for two months. The Army tries hard to forward mail to the men in the field, but by spring we're going to be on the move every day, from what I hear. But I can still write to you in Cincinnati, I hope," Lester wanted to make sure.

"Do you want me to hold for you any mail sent to my address here in Cincinnati?" she offered.

Lester readily accepted, "That would make me feel connected to a spot on this earth for the first time in two years! And a spot in the North at that! The only people who might write me are my mother, Lorna McGill, in Knoxville, and a friend I hope to locate some day, named Jake. I can probably reconnect with my mother now that she's safe where she is, but I don't know how I'll find Jake."

"Was he a school friend?" Gretchen seemed genuinely interested.

"No, Jake is a man about my age who just escaped slavery a year ago and was intending to enlist in the U.S.C.T.," Lester studied her reaction. She exhibited no surprise but instead wanted to hear the whole story of Lester's escape from Tennessee with Jake's invaluable aid.

"If you ever find him after the war, I hope I'll meet him," she assured Lester.

By the time Lester had to rejoin his regiment, he had formed the image in his mind of a peaceful existence in Cincinnati with Gretchen and surrounded by friends. These visions of home would have to sustain him through another year of war.

Chapter 7
Raising Hell in Georgia

Camp Nelson had served a number of purposes over the course of the war. Situated near Lexington, it had once served as a refugee camp with a sketchy history in its behavior toward Black refugees. When Lester arrived, he was impressed with the acres of buildings across its expansive grounds on the Kentucky River. It was by no accident that a mounted unit be organized in the heart of Kentucky's horse country. The U.S. Army seemed willing to grant contracts to any reliable supplier – in this case, of horses. Horses were purchased for cavalry service until they were in need of rehabilitation on the same farms. Those successfully restored to fit condition were then returned to duty.

Lester on a horse

As men returned from furlough, Colonel Croxton moved them to the suburbs of Lexington. There they were officially named 4th Kentucky Mounted Infantry. This was the designation given to a unit that used horses for mobility but fought dismounted with infantry shoulder arms. The weapons furnished in Lexington were breech-loading carbines, the same as cavalry was using. This carbine fired a modern metallic cartridge, which the South was unable to manufacture. A mounted infantry unit can be trained in less time than true cavalry. In both cases, the soldier devoted much time to the care of his horse while the infantry could loll in camp at the end of the day.

When the men arrived at their new camp, they resumed their customary chatter. There was a lot to talk about, starting with their experiences in the peaceful setting of their homes. To some, the home town had changed so much in three years that they had little in common with people they had once known well. Towns with some families harboring Confederate sentiments could make a man feel uncomfortable while coming home. Married men usually came back to camp wishing that the idyllic days at home could have lasted longer. Lester waited to relate his Cincinnati experience until he was comfortably adjusted to life in the new camp.

"So much change in just a few weeks," he said to himself. "A new place to call home, training for mounted service, a new camp, and many new comrades being absorbed from disbanded regiments; we don't even know what we'll be doing next." He kept details of his time spent with Gretchen to himself, since the experience was so new to him that he didn't want to sound foolish.

There was soon more change to deal with when it was announced that President Lincoln had again shuffled his high command. The announcement led to new speculation over the next assignment. The men listened intently as the message was relayed, "The President will promote Major General Grant to the rank of Lieutenant General and place him in command of all U.S. armies. General Sherman replaces Grant in command of the Western theater. General Thomas will retain command of the Army of the Cumberland, currently in winter camp at Chattanooga. General Halleck will now report to General Grant as his chief-of-staff in Washington."

The 4th Kentucky troopers still had few clues about their next assignment once they were ready to leave camp. One opinion was advanced by Hubert, who had surprised everyone when he showed up at Camp Nelson, having chosen to reenlist. He was one of many whose experience at home was a disappointment. He had hoped people would pay attention to him when he showed up in his home town, but his uniform didn't improve his visibility. He now hoped he'd appear taller on a horse, so he reluctantly returned to his unit to make the most of whatever lay ahead. His hopes for limited combat clearly hadn't diminished when he ventured, "Lincoln wants Grant in the East because that's where the war needs to be won. He'll throw everything he has against Lee in order to take Richmond by November. There won't be enough left for us, so we'll be on occupation duty out here in the backwoods."

Lester pointed out that command in the West had been vested in Sherman, a man Grant would never employ in a secondary role. "No," he assured Hubert, "Something big will be expected of us. It should be obvious that Sherman has his eyes on Atlanta, and the newspapers that we get from Nashville say Bragg's been replaced by Joe Johnston. He's a smarter opponent, popular with his men because he favors maneuver over fighting and doesn't run up casualties the way Lee does."

Wilbur, as usual, painted a broader context of the war. "We have over 110,000 experienced men assembled in camps all around central Tennessee under proven generals. The only battle the Rebs have won in the West was Chickamauga after Bragg was heavily reinforced with troops from Virginia. Where does Johnston find more troops? If Grant takes on Lee in Virginia, Johnston is on his own. Davis can't afford to let go of Atlanta; it's the heart of his war industry. Atlanta, Selma, Montgomery, Augusta, Macon – they're all connected. Davis can't keep up a two-front war forever."

Grrr's opinion had to do with Sherman, "I wasn't too impressed with Sherman's fighting at Missionary Ridge. Thomas had to come to his rescue."

Wilbur went on, "I was talking with some men from an Iowa regiment about Sherman's January drive from Vicksburg into the interior of Mississippi. He destroyed the railroads in his path and burned anything else of military value before torching much of Meridian and its railroad center. Then he marched back to Vicksburg, causing more ruin. He has hit Jackson three times by now and most of Mississippi is out of the war. The whole East bank of the river is full of contraband camps and government farms. Apparently Sherman knows how to hit the Rebels where it hurts."

"I hope Sherman brings his matches to Georgia," cracked Jasper.

"Much will be expected of Sherman," Wilbur continued. "What Captain Latrobe told us is true. When I was on furlough in Ohio, war-weariness was getting worse. The Democrats will nominate a peace candidate who will claim the war cannot be won."

Jasper suggested, "They should nominate McClellan! He's good at not winning!" Someone reminded him that McClellan was one of the candidates being considered and most of the men expressed disapproval. Soldiers in the West had little use for Eastern generals and McClellan especially.

Talk eventually shifted to the practicalities of a major advance on Atlanta. "Everyone knows an army travels on its stomach," noted Hubert. "Up to now, we've always fit close to our base of supply. It has to be a hundred miles to Atlanta with no river, just a single track."

Grrr added, "We'll have Forrest's and Wheeler's cavalry raiding behind us. It will take half our men just to protect our supply line!"

When the men retired for the night, their minds were occupied with logistical challenges, a general new to independent command, and a hostile Deep South that could swallow an army whole.

Moving south

The 4th Kentucky Mounted Infantry reached Chattanooga shortly after Sherman had begun his advance on Atlanta. The men marveled at the immensity of military assets that Sherman was bringing up to support his operations. He had co-opted the private railroads in Tennessee for military use so that a steady stream of supplies reached the forces under his command. Even Wilbur marveled at the logistical genius displayed by Sherman in his preparations and operations. Supply depots along the line of advance, stockpiled rails and cross-ties, prefabricated bridge trusses, specially trained repair crews, and blockhouses with guards at the bridges showed that Sherman had neglected nothing. His entire force consisted of three armies, an *army group* as it were. The Army of the Cumberland under Thomas was the largest. Next came the Army of the Tennessee under James McPherson, and the smallest was John Schofield's 1-corps Army of the Ohio, the second to be so named.

The 4th Kentucky was directed into camp about ten miles from Lafayette, Georgia. This was the regiment's base while it patrolled and protected a section of Sherman's vital rail line. There were some minor skirmishes with Confederate raiders, but nothing that could be called a pitched battle. Northern Georgia already presented a dismal appearance. The terrain was hilly, with several ridges running across the Union line of advance. These offered Johnston defensive positions from which he could slow Sherman's advancing forces. The land was best suited for small farms, since the soil did not lend itself to cotton cultivation. Lester saw very little prosperity in this region. Most of what grew there had already been foraged by Confederates or the many armed bands that roamed at will. Of the few slaves who lived in that region, a number had fled to Chattanooga.

Guarding Sherman's supply line involved numerous patrols and scouting missions. Some ranged far from the railroad and beyond the flanks of the infantry columns. In northern Georgia, men in the 4th Kentucky learned about the hardships of war from the rural poor in the region. Sergeant Morrow led his detachment along rutted backcountry roads past dwellings where the inhabitants were barely hanging on. The families consisted largely of women and small children, the only men present being aged or infirm. Lester stopped to talk with two farm women and three children who, he guessed, ranged in age from five to nine. The youngest was the most shabbily-clad, probably wearing the brother's hand-me-downs. The girl was showing signs of malnutrition in her pallid complexion and a sunken, vacant look in her light-blue eyes. The older woman told Lester, "We been trying to grow a few root crops for food, but we're learning to make food from anything that crawls or grows on this ground."

"We're glad to see all you men in blue finally show up," she went on. "The Secesh soldiers keep coming through to hunt deserters and boys who don't want to fight for the planters. The hills are full of Lincolnites. They operate secretly to get Rebels to desert and slaves to escape. Soldiers sent in to catch them sometimes don't back come out. All the men who were neighbors have disappeared into the mountains."

"I hope your men return in good health when this is over. Meanwhile, most of Georgia will be cleared of Confederates once General Sherman drives them out of Atlanta," Lester assured her.

"Every time soldiers pull out, this land is crawling with thieves who prey on the helpless folk. You can't tell me you boys will stay to protect us once the armies move south," the lady stated the truth. Lester knew this woman's apprehensions would soon become reality all over the South.

Sherman's advance consisted of a series of flanking maneuvers, each resulting in Johnston falling back to a new line of defense. The one major offensive ordered by Sherman was an ill-advised attack against *Kennesaw Mountain*, which met with a costly repulse. After another flanking movement put Sherman across the Chattahoochee River, he was little more than ten miles from the fortified city of Atlanta. Sherman's men found this area abundant with food and practiced unauthorized forage after the sparse country they had just come through. The 4th Kentucky joined the main force on the west bank of the Chattahoochee, where it was brigaded with three regiments of regular cavalry. Croxton, having recovered from his Chickamauga wound, was once again brigade commander, with a new rank of brigadier general. The divisional commander was Edward McCook. It felt strange for an infantry unit to be mixed in with true cavalry.

Once across the river, Sherman had no more natural barriers between his forces and Atlanta. It was soon learned that Davis had replaced Johnston with John Bell Hood, aggressive but deficient in all other qualities expected of a general. When he took over, he withdrew his army into the works that surrounded the city. Sherman, though, knew that Hood would come out and fight. First he struck Thomas's army on July 20 while it was crossing *Peach Tree Creek* and was repulsed with heavy losses. Hood then struck McPherson east of the city two days later, resulting in the *Battle of Atlanta* and another repulse while the railroad coming from the east was destroyed. As Sherman swung west of town, Hood attacked at *Ezra Church* and again failed with losses he could not replace.

On July 27, Sherman sent two divisions of cavalry (Edward McCook's and George Stoneman's) on a mission to wreck the Atlanta and Montgomery Railroad, and then the Macon and Western Railroad. Both tracks ran in from the south, merging a few miles before reaching Atlanta, and were the only two lines remaining to feed Hood's army. Orders to the widely separated cavalry commanders instructed them to converge on Lovejoy Station, on the Macon road, and destroy several miles of track. Lester was excited about his first real cavalry raid, but soon the excitement turned to humiliation. McCook's division destroyed a small stretch of the Atlanta and Montgomery tracks before he went on to meet Stoneman. Unexpectedly, Stoneman decided to play hero by rescuing Union P.O.W.'s from Andersonville Prison. He was still far from the prison when he was struck by Joe Wheeler's much larger cavalry force. Stoneman and a large portion of his division were captured. Since McCook's 3,500 were about to be outnumbered, they began to retire west to Union camps, but had to fight a running battle. The division broke up into scattered groups trying to reach safety on the other side of the Chattahoochee. McCook lost over a thousand men, most taken prisoner. The remnants of the 4th Kentucky straggled into Marietta in August, having lost almost half their number to capture. Sherman finally had to accept that effective destruction of railroads required a large force of infantry.

The survivors of Croxton's brigade were sent to Kingston, further north on the railroad, for reorganization. They went into camp there until

September 17. Lester had lost some companions, including Grrr and Hubert, reported captured. They were fighting near the town of Newnan as they tried to reach the river. The Confederates were holding their prisoners under guard until a train could arrive and transfer them to Andersonville. It was a bitter experience for a regiment so proud of its service as infantry, only to be so badly squandered as horsemen.

"It's no wonder that Sherman has little regard for cavalry. What we need, if this war goes on, is a competent leader. Grant has Sheridan commanding a corps in the East and he's killed Jeb Stuart outside of Richmond. And here we are -- four separate divisions and we can't even coordinate a simple railroad raid," Wilbur sounded bitter.

Here in Kingston, news reached camp that on September 1, Sherman had brought most of his infantry against the Macon and West Point Railroad at Jonesboro, near Lovejoy Station. The badly outnumbered Hood was unable to drive Sherman away from the railroad and soon he would be starved out if he did not evacuate the city that night. When Sherman heard a huge explosion in Atlanta, he knew it was Hood's ammunition train, intentionally ignited to deny it to the Yankees. The first of Sherman's troops marched into Atlanta on September 2. Their colorful accounts spread through Sherman's armies. When they entered, they found some of the city destroyed by Hood's train explosion and some by the artillery barrage in the weeks leading up to this day. Most of the civilians who fled Atlanta had already done so earlier in the summer. Of those who remained, some civilians stayed inside their homes, but much of the city's population– deserters, stragglers, convicts, refugees, whether slave or free, young or old -- looted the Confederate commissary stores for food, clothing, whiskey, anything they could carry away. Union soldiers usually refrained from entering occupied homes, but some were not always that considerate.

A week after taking possession, Sherman issued an order requiring nearly all remaining civilians to vacate Atlanta. It was to be a military base for his armies and he could not feed or protect residents. Rail transportation was furnished to those choosing to go North. For those wishing to remain in the South, they were given safe conduct beyond Union lines. Not surprisingly, most of the newly-emancipated eagerly piled on the northbound trains. When Lester was told of the evictions of formerly wealthy Atlanta citizens who became homeless refugees, he wondered what became of Hannah's parents. He doubted that Slade Clifton would choose to go north. By now, Lester was glad to be in Kingston where he did not have to witness the misery of Atlanta's displaced citizens.

Escape and rescue

The days of relative leisure in Kingston found the men experiencing mixed thoughts about their current role. They were dissatisfied with their use as cavalry and resented the ineptitude of cavalry officers. Stoneman was a cast-off from the East and their own divisional commander, Ed McCook, was ineffective. This was the first time the 4th Kentucky was not somewhere in Thomas's chain of command and they missed Old Pap. Wilbur reminded them that the only man senior to McCook was General Sherman. "Uncle Billy has handled this army skillfully and brought us all the way to Atlanta. We might do better after this if our cavalry had a skilled corps commander. Then we could stand a chance against Wheeler or Forrest."

One night while the men were cooking their rations, they were startled by the appearance of two soldiers in soiled uniforms who approached the campfire. Confusion turned to disbelief to glee when Jasper shouted, "Hubert! Grrr!" They had managed to break free of their captors near Newnan. Their account of the escape held everyone's attention till they had covered every last detail.

Grrr began, "After our brigade dissolved into groups, eight of us got surrounded a mile or so from Newnan. They were planning to hold all of us in a warehouse till they repaired the track on the Montgomery railroad after we worked so hard to wreck it the day before. Combined with about thirty others, we were herded down a road through the woods when one man broke and ran into the trees. I guess we all thought it was a good idea because everybody scattered in all directions. I knew they couldn't catch all of us, so I went in the direction that looked to have tree cover too thick for a horse to penetrate."

Hubert picked up from there, "I could hear Rebels shouting and firing and I tried to stay ahead of the noise. Picturing myself in Andersonville gave me energy I never knew I had. But then this Rebel suddenly jumps out in front of me and cuts me off with his carbine leveled at my chest. I stood there staring at this backwoods rube with yellow teeth and thought I saw the carbine's hammer resting on a spent cap. I was debating whether to grab the muzzle when the Reb suddenly collapsed to the ground at my feet. And there stands Grrr holding a rock the size of a paving stone with the Rebel's brains dripping from it. We kept moving as best we could, ducking in and out of tree cover. Now we were two soldiers lost in the middle of Nowhere, Georgia."

"We had to stop and rest when the sun went down," Grrr took over. "I wondered if they used bloodhounds to track escapees like they do with runaway slaves. We weren't sure what to do but we had to keep covering ground. We could tell we were still heading west by the artillery fire outside Atlanta coming from our right. There was just enough daylight left to make out an old farm with what we figured were a few acres of cotton. The house was kind of run-down and not too big. There was a few slave cabins in back with a cooking fire where people were cooking supper. I thought Hubert had lost his mind when he suggested we could find help there."

"I remembered what Lester told me about P.O.W.'s rescued by slaves, so we agreed to take a chance," Hubert said as he smiled in Lester's direction. "There were a few adults sitting near the fire. We approached cautiously and tried not to startle them, so we whispered, 'Northern soldiers' before we came too close. 'Can you help us?' They were like magic words. They saw our blue uniforms and soon we were fed some hearty soup with vegetables from their garden -- better than army rations. Next they showed us a shed where we could hide for the night. The eldest man told us, 'It's too dark to go anywhere tonight, but you're safe here till morning. Then a guide will lead you to the river.' Right at dawn, a young girl came to where we were sleeping and told us to follow her. She could not have been older than ten. She took us from one woodlot to another, so we never had to risk being out in the open. Late in the day, she took us to the edge of a field that she said fronted on a road, but we couldn't cross it safely until dark. She said the river was just beyond the road and if we went straight to it, we should be able to see the U.S. picket fire on the opposite bank. We should find a small boat hidden in the brush to row across to the pickets."

"Her knowledge had been good so far, so we went as she said," Grrr resumed. "We didn't see the picket fire when we hit the river, but after we followed the river north a ways, it came into view. When we were directly across from it, a man whispered from the reeds that he was with the boat. 'We had to make sure you were the soldiers we expected,' he told us. His fellow passengers were a young slave woman and her child. We were relieved when the five of us made it to the other side in that wreck of a boat. The man told us, 'I'm not going ashore with you. As soon as you're on land, I'm taking this boat back to be used again.'"

"The mother added, 'I was wanting to escape with my baby for some time now, but we heard some of Sherman's men don't want us around. I thought we'd have a better chance if we went across with you soldiers.' They never told us how they came to expect us. Nobody even wanted to tell us their name. Everything is kept secret, like the Underground Railroad. It's how people survive, I guess."

Hubert finished the saga, "Once we made it across, the pickets told us that more of McCook's division had crossed at several points and was regrouping in Marietta. The officers there said they would take proper care of our free friends. The brigade had been sent here to Kingston by then. We couldn't wait to rejoin you."

As Lester listened intently to Grrr and Hubert, he could tell that both had been profoundly influenced by the experience of the past few days. Grrr was coming around to appreciate the valuable allies he had in the slave community. He seemed more subdued and cheerful than before. For Hubert, the experience of capture by what he described as Wheeler's *half-crazed Rebel tribe* steeled him for the next campaign. He talked excitedly about pitching into the next Confederate cavalry they saw. The enthusiasm would have to get him through the rest of the war. From now on, the 4th Kentucky Mounted would be up against Nathan Bedford Forrest.

The Northern newspapers, usually detested by Sherman, patriotically touted the capture of Atlanta as validation of the Union Army's strategy. Ironically, three days earlier, the Democratic Convention had nominated George McClellan on a peace platform. Sherman was well-aware that propaganda value of a military success is fleeting. He had no further use for Atlanta beyond its capture and destruction of its war resources. Still, President Lincoln and Grant told him not to undertake any risky actions until after the election. When November arrived, Lincoln won in an electoral landslide, winning over 70% of the soldier vote, a franchise granted to most soldiers that year.

The supply line coming in from Chattanooga remained open only through much exertion in countering Hood's army every time he attacked the railroad. When bits of information filtered through the Union ranks, men in the 4th Kentucky once again had to call on Wilbur to explain what was about to happen.

"I've been hearing that Sherman is splitting his forces. He's taking four corps of infantry and a division of cavalry on a march through enemy country. Hood is moving in the opposite direction, so General Thomas was sent to Nashville where he'll deal with Hood if he tries to go north," Wilbur began.

"What can Hood possibly accomplish?" Grrrr wondered. "Does Thomas have enough men?"

Wilbur sighed, "I hope so, especially since we'll be serving under Thomas again."

The men were all pleased to hear that.

Hubert couldn't wait to ask, "What cavalry is Sherman taking on his march? I wish we could go. It sounds like an ideal campaign – a triumphant march." Hubert never looked so motivated.

"I heard his cavalry will be led by Judson Kilpatrick, another Eastern discard. We should be glad we're not under him. Someone said Grant calls him *a damned fool*."

"Every cavalry commander we've seen so far fits that description," Jasper pointed out. "I hope Croxton still commands our brigade."

"He does," Wilbur assured him. "And we're being consolidated into a cavalry corps under James Wilson. Remember that protégé on Grant's staff at Chattanooga? Grant took him to Virginia and converted him to cavalry. I think Grant sent him here because our cavalry has been poorly led."

"How do we know he's any better?" challenged Grrr.

"Well, he's only four years out of West Point and already a major general leading a corps of 12,000 troopers at age 27. He's one of the boy generals, like George Custer," Wilbur submitted. "Grant must know Wilson pretty well after three years, and Grant would not send us another castoff, not with Forrest on the loose."

Total War

It was November 15 when Sherman marched his high-spirited army out of Atlanta, bound for a destination known only to his top generals. His four corps of infantry marched in parallel routes, along a front fifty to sixty miles wide. Kilpatrick had selected the best mounts for his cavalry and left enough horses to mount only a fraction of Wilson's corps. In an unusual move, Sherman attached the *1st Alabama Cavalry* to his headquarters as his escort across Georgia. The regiment was composed of 2,000 men, mostly from northern Alabama, who formed their own U.S. regiment to serve the Union. Every Confederate state except South Carolina contributed enough men to fill at least one U.S. regiment.

Sherman's intent was to further the process of exhausting the Confederacy. Much of the South was already feeling the devastation of war by 1864. Now under the Grant – Sherman strategy, the work of exhaustion was intensified. Phillip Sheridan had burned out the Shenandoah Valley that fall, depriving Lee of the chief source of food for his army and destitute civilians. Sherman targeted factories, machine shops, warehouses, transportation infrastructure, and crops in the field – anything to weaken the Confederacy. Material damage was the most visible, but a more insidious target was Southern morale, both within the armies and at home. By the time Sherman reached the Atlantic near Savannah at Christmas, he had left in his wake almost three-hundred miles of desolation and proof to Southern civilians their armies could do nothing to stop the Yankees no matter where they chose to go.

Chapter 8
End of the Cause in Tennessee

Sherman knew when he started out on his march that Hood's army was preparing to set out on a fool's errand into central Tennessee. Hood marched north across Alabama, moving toward a crossing of the Tennessee River. There he was to meet with Forrest's cavalry, which had been raiding further north. From there, they were to advance on Nashville. Thomas was not given much time to consolidate the various infantry units as they came into Nashville and then organize them for battle. The two corps that Sherman sent him from Atlanta were commanded by John Schofield, who was ordered to delay Hood's advance. Most of Wilson's cavalry was without mounts or repeating carbines, but the 4th Kentucky Mounted and the three regiments of regular cavalry in Croxton's brigade were provided with suitable mounts. They were sent to northern Alabama to cooperate in Schofield's delaying action.

Lester and his fellow horsemen described all of northern Alabama as a desecrated land, with many houses reduced to charred stand-alone chimneys and ruins of walls defying gravity. Residents watched Hood's soldiers trudging north. The sight of ill-equipped, poorly-clad, malnourished scarecrows on a forlorn venture did little to generate a sense of optimism in those who cheered them on anyway. All the civilians could give was support in a moral sense; there was no food or material support left.

Hood linked up with Forrest's cavalry on November 19 at Florence, Alabama, where they crossed the Tennessee River. Croxton's brigade was credited with delaying Hood's crossing, giving Schofield additional time to deploy his infantry. Over the next few days, the two armies tried to outmaneuver each other along a route that ran north through Tennessee towns of Pulaski, Columbia, Spring Hill, Franklin, and Nashville. Schofield was almost trapped at Spring Hill, but a night march enabled him to slip past Hood and take a fortified position at Franklin, with his back to the Harpeth River where the bridge had been destroyed. Schofield was in the process of bridging the river and putting his wagons across when Hood approached the works. Hood ordered a series of suicidal frontal assaults that continued until well after dark. During the fighting, Croxton's brigade and any other cavalry that Wilson could mount performed impressively in frustrating Forrest's efforts to ford the Harpeth and fall on Schofield's rear and line of retreat.

Nashville IV: Citadel for a gathering host

During the night, Schofield withdrew his forces across the Harpeth to complete the march to Nashville. In the morning, the men in Hood's army surveyed the ghastly scene, with bodies lying in heaps where they fell outside the now-vacant Franklin works. The fiasco cost Hood over 6,000 casualties, three times the number lost by Schofield. Still, he moved his army to Nashville and entrenched a line south of the formidable Union fortifications. Hood's poorly supplied and ill-equipped men suffered severely for much of the time in the freezing weather.

The army in Nashville that Thomas commanded did not have a name. He had infantry corps from three different armies as well as a large provisional division under Benjamin Steedman, made up of garrison troops, new recruits, and two brigades of U.S.C.T. volunteers. Wilson's cavalry went into camp on the north side of the Cumberland River. In order to mount his troopers, Wilson was given permission to sweep through the surrounding area and impress any horses that were suitable for cavalry use. Lester took advantage of the time spent on preparations to stroll through Nashville and observe how much it had changed this time. He figured there was a chance he might find Jake among the regiments camped there if he had in fact enlisted under the Clifton surname.

Lester first made his way to the drugstore where he knew he had a relative in Cyrus Duncan. On entering the shop, he saw a Union officer talking with a lady who was standing behind the counter. When they turned to look toward the doorway, Lester first saw the insignia of a major on one and a familiar face on the other.

He simultaneously saluted and exclaimed, "Mother!"

As it turned out, Major Connor had been serving in Knoxville since Burnside's occupation. He met Lester's mother Lorna while Longstreet had the city under siege. She was one of several volunteers working in support of the soldiers. The two became friends there – so much so that when General Thomas pulled in troops from various garrisons to defend

Nashville, Major Connor agreed to bring her with him on the train.

The major was not at all condescending toward Lester, the private. He had been a staff officer in the Knoxville garrison and now he was adjutant to one of the generals under Steedman. After a few minutes of pleasant conversation, the major shook Lester's hand as he was leaving. He told Lester he had a healthy respect for the enlisted men and the way they always get the job done. To Lester, he seemed to be auditioning for the role of step-father.

"I'll give you and your mother some privacy while you get reacquainted after all this time. Let me know if there's anything I can do for you," the major offered.

This unexpected gesture seemed sincere enough for Lester to ask, "Is there some way to locate a man in the U.S.C.T.? He probably enlisted in Nashville, but I don't know where his regiment is serving. His name is Jake, and he may be using the surname *Clifton*. He came in from Scott County after Kirby Smith went off on his invasion of Kentucky."

"If he's serving in Nashville, the brigade and regimental commanders may be able to find him on the muster rolls," Major Connor sounded encouraging. "It may take some time, but there have to be papers somewhere in the confused records kept by the Army."

Lester felt that, in a way, his life was coming back together. He was reunited with his mother, he'd met his cousin Cyrus, and now there was a possibility of finding his friend Jake.

"It would be perfect if, after we destroy Hood's army, I can serve out my enlistment here in Nashville," he told his mother. "I had been trying to convince myself that you were safe in Knoxville, but merely being safe is not much of a life. It's such a relief to find you out of the upper valley, plus keeping company with an officer gentleman. Meanwhile, are you living comfortably here?"

"I've been helping Cousin Cyrus here in the store. My living quarters upstairs are roomy and comfortable. The city has been under military control for over two years and now it's filling up with more soldiers than I ever saw. Most long-time residents in Nashville are full of resentment toward Northerners. Now they see former slaves in blue uniforms, carrying muskets. Their whole world has been up-ended. They know how George Thomas can fight and expect him to drive Hood back into Alabama," she reported.

"The talk in camp is that high command is preparing to destroy Hood's army here in Nashville. There can't be any western Confederate army left in the field once the battle is over," Lester assured her.

"Does Hood have any chance? Why is he even here? His men must be freezing out there," as she echoed the thoughts of the other Unionists in Nashville.

"Hood is sacrificing a generation of Southern manhood to prove his own. His reckless charges confuse courage with pride. Too many Rebels want to go down fighting for a lost cause and will follow Hood to their own end in some burial mound. It's a shame we have to risk our own lives in sending Hood's army to its doom. But right now I want to learn more about Major Connor. He seemed genuine for an officer," Lester said to show approval of his mother's new friend.

She looked pleased as she told her son, "I was hoping you'd accept him. When the volunteer army is mustered out, if the war ever ends, we plan to be married in Indianapolis, where his family has a large dry goods business. The sooner you take care of Hood, the sooner we can leave Tennessee."

"I wonder if anybody will be left in Tennessee when this is over. The whole state is dotted with desolated farmlands, burned-out towns, abandoned buildings and houses, and limited means of supporting life," sighed the young man who had never been out of Tennessee until the war.

"The vacant Clifton place was vandalized by anti-secessionists several times. Last I heard of Hannah, she couldn't leave the South soon enough. She was working here in a contraband camp, but she really wanted to attend school in the North. She told people she was trying to lose her regional accent. One of the women she knew in the Sanitary Commission said Hannah was talking about a school in Ohio that calls itself coeducational. Its name is Oberlin College," she told him. "The Clifton slaves disappeared right after Burnside occupied the upper valley. Now, I'm afraid it's one big guerrilla war and will stay that way long after the war."

"I'm thinking of making it at least as far as Cincinnati myself," Lester informed her in a voice that was turning increasingly cheerful. "I spent most of my furlough there keeping company with a lady named Gretchen. Her father has a job for me in his plant if I choose to make my home there. Gretchen and I correspond when the Army Post Office knows where I am. She offered to hold any mail sent to her address in

Cincinnati. I want to give you that address now. If the major finds Jake, encourage him to write me there too. I think we can find him better employment in Cincinnati than anything here. Once we crush Hood, the cavalry will be expected to pursue him and run him into the ground. Soon's we do that, I'll write to let you know where we're camped. Right now, I'm expected in Wilson's camp. So happy to see you, Mother!"

As Lester crossed to the north side of the river, he thought about the promising life awaiting him if he should manage to survive the end of the war. He would soon be in battle against the pathetic remnants of the Army of Tennessee, that army his comrades had been fighting since 1861, when it was commanded by Albert Sidney Johnson.

"Still," he told himself, "a mounted man makes a good target. I hope this ends the war in the West."

A disheartened rabble

The battle plan that Thomas developed called for Wilson's cavalry corps to serve an active combat role in the attack on Hood's left flank. Once the flank was turned, Wilson would next block the only possible Confederate lines of retreat and further damage Hood in pursuit. It was not until December 8 that Wilson managed to mount three divisions plus Croxton's oversized brigade and arm them with 7-shot Spencer carbines. Just at the last moment, though, a fierce storm brought freezing rain that coated the ground with a thick layer of ice that precluded any movement of troops. It also added to the suffering of Hood's men. Everyone was growing impatient, including Grant back in Virginia, who was not fully aware of conditions in Nashville and nearly removed Thomas. At last, December 15 brought in a warm front that melted the ice and allowed Thomas to begin the attack.

Lester and the rest of the 4th Kentucky Mounted saddled up and took position on the right flank of Thomas's line. Excitement ran through the regiment in what would be their first offensive battle as cavalry. Thomas's tactical plan called for a *grand left wheel*, with three infantry corps forming an advancing front that would pivot on its left, then swing like a door to fall on Hood's thinly-defended left flank. Heavy morning fog resulted in infantry brigades being misdirected and obstructing the path of Wilson's cavalry. The assault was delayed, but once adjustments were made and the Union line advanced, it came slamming into Hood's left as planned. The Confederates had tried to anchor their left with a series of five *redoubts*, which are enclosed artillery positions with infantry support. These proved inadequate as Federal infantry and dismounted cavalry captured them one-by-one. Thomas's infantry was rolling up the Confederate left against weak resistance, resulting in fewer casualties than in most battles. With the winter solstice only days away, the early darkness ended the day's fighting before Thomas could finish off his foe.

During the night, Hood pulled his army back over a mile and shortened his line so that each flank was anchored on a sizeable hill. The fighting had not been as savage as others experienced by the 4th Kentucky. The Rebels seemed to be missing the spirit that had defined them in the past. Most of their losses this day were through surrender or desertion. The night was cold as the men slept on their arms, but it seemed to Lester that the successes on the first day of battle had left his comrades oblivious to the temperature. To a man, the 4th Kentucky hoped that Hood would not retreat during the night.

Thomas used the early morning to organize his attacking force. Action began with another diversion against Hood's right, its flank resting on the well-fortified Overton Hill. The force that attacked Overton Hill included several U.S.C.T. regiments. Although the works were not captured, the assault was so convincing that Hood significantly weakened other sectors of his line to reinforce the right. The valor exhibited by the U.S.C.T. units was noted by all who witnessed their performance on the battlefield. Reports of the action changed the attitudes and opinions of many in the U.S. Army and government, as did earlier actions reported from *Milliken's Bend* in Louisiana and *Fort Wagner* in South Carolina.

When the main attack struck the Confederate left, anchored on Shy's Hill, Wilson's cavalry rode around the flank. Some brigades took positions where they could obstruct the expected retreat, while Croxton joined others who dismounted and approached Shy's Hill from the rear (south). The works on the hill were subjected to artillery fire from three directions while infantry advanced from the north and west. Lester and every soldier on the battlefield could see the Confederate colors fall on that hill as the whole of Hood's line, from its left to its right, fled the field, having lost most of its cohesion. Some tried to conduct an orderly retreat, while many surrendered or took advantage of the confusion to desert. Hood had left much of his artillery, his wounded, supplies, and wagons, while soldiers littered the road with unneeded gear. Thomas referred to these soldiers in flight as *a disheartened rabble*.

Pursuit of a defeated enemy after battle usually resulted in little damage and allowed the beaten army to maintain some organization. In this instance, though, Thomas's objective was not merely to repulse Hood's army, but to end its existence. Wilson's assignment in this phase of the battle was to impede Hood's retreat to give the infantry time to come up and further weaken the Rebels. After the pursuit began, swollen rivers, bridges gone, and a rear-guard action by Forrest's cavalry kept alive this pitiful remnant of the once-proud Army of Tennessee. When its retreat ended in Tupelo, Mississippi, only around 15,000 remained in the ranks and half of these were deemed unfit for further service.

The 4th Kentucky had fought this once second-largest Confederate army since Mill Springs, Thomas's first victory. They had followed George Thomas all through the war and now to his offensive masterpiece at Nashville. Except for small, scattered units, there was no Confederacy west of the Appalachians. Georgia, too, was no longer under the military control of Richmond. News of Sherman's arrival on the Atlantic Coast outside Savannah and his occupation of the city on Christmas, 1864 without a fight were celebrated throughout the U.S. Army. Citizens in Savannah were gratified with the respect shown by the soldiers during their month of rest and resupplying in preparation for the next campaign – in the Carolinas.

Chapter 9
Coup de Grâce in Alabama

The pursuit of Hood's remnants officially ended at the Tennessee River on December 26. Wilson's exhausted men on jaded mounts were sent to the northwestern corner of Alabama near Waterloo, on the river just downstream from Muscle Shoals. There the cavalry corps remained until March 22, wondering whether the Army would give them another assignment. While Wilson kept them busy in camp, Thomas was directed to send his three infantry corps to active theaters and to maintain a garrison in Nashville. As the 4th Kentucky made itself comfortable in camp, there was much speculation over why the Army was remounting and rearming close to 15,000 experienced, superbly-led cavalrymen. There had to be an operation in the works that would require a swift, yet powerful mounted force of this size.

"We ran off all the Rebels from these parts when Hood limped away," Grrr claimed. "From Kentucky to Mississippi to here, all we see are refugees coming from land stripped bare of food crowding into towns already full of starving civilians. They don't need our cavalry; they need a meal." The men were surprised by the recent signs of humanity in the normally hostile Grrr.

Food and all other supplies needed by Wilson's cavalry were abundant in camp. The Tennessee was navigable in all seasons from the Ohio upstream as far as Muscle Shoals. Except for mail call, the arrival of the sutler's wagon with a new supply of goods was the most welcome event in camp. The Army allowed entrepreneurs to run a store on wheels that sold goods to soldiers. A sutlery could carry any number of goods needed by the men, including newspapers, stationery, canned food items, candles, sewing needs, playing cards, tobacco, lucifers (matches), personal care products, and books.

After one visit to the sutler's tent, Grrr grumbled to is messmates. "Too bad he don't sell baseballs. Nobody here is playing the game. Probably 'cause there's no Northern regiments in the cavalry."

"It shows how desperate the men are to break up the boredom of camp," Wilbur complained. "Adults amusing themselves with a child's game."

Lester agreed, "I was watching some boys playing ball in Cincinnati. I have to admit it's entertaining to watch. Once the war is over, I doubt we'll see adults with the time to play ball. They have to earn a living."

Jasper contributed another product of his imagination, "If it's fun to watch, people might pay to attend a game. Then teams could pay a salary to the best players."

Lester smiled, "That might work in the gentlemen's clubs of New England, but Cincinnati is a hard-workin' city. No time for child's games."

Jasper wouldn't let it go, "What if they sold beer to the spectators? And food?" It was at points like this that someone would change the subject.

Newspapers passed through dozens of hands in camp. Sometimes a small group gathered to listen to one of the more literate men read the news. Freedom of the press was mostly honored in the North and opinionated editors exercised this right to the fullest. Generals always made good targets, though opinions could swing overnight from condemnation to lavish praise if the next battle went well. General Sherman had been unmercifully criticized in the Northern papers, but after taking Atlanta, he was nearly worshipped by the Republicans for his influence on Mr. Lincoln's reelection. The newspapers reported Sherman to be marching his reinvigorated army through South Carolina, inflicting even greater devastation than visited on Georgia. As Hubert was listening to this account, his expression showed how he was still bemoaning that the 4th Kentucky was not chosen to go on the adventure of a lifetime.

It was another bleak holiday season for men so far from home. At first, the men found winter camp to be a welcome break from the past year's exertions, but as 1865 entered February, the inactivity was making some impatient to go home. Men in the 4th Kentucky couldn't figure out why they were so far from active military operations. "I was enjoying mounted service," Hubert said, "even chasing Hood all the way to the Tennessee. I hope they send us somewhere to show what we can do."

Lester told him that was unlikely. "The South will soon have to accept the unavoidable facts and admit defeat. You've seen the civilians every place we pass through. They can't even support themselves, let alone an army. There's no safe place anymore. The whole South is a tragic mix of refugees, roving outlaw bands, guerrillas, deserters, Union partisans, vigilantes, and probably types we haven't seen yet."

"Yesterday I rode a short distance back from the river," Grrr reported. "You wouldn't believe what families do just to survive. They get no flour, greens, meat, or much else. People make bread out of potatoes and coffee out of wild peas. Folks in the uplands can't hunt or fish 'cause they got no ammunition or fishhooks. People are eating insects, snakes, rats."

"That's what they mean by *states' rats*!" Jasper snickered.

Grrr ignored that and added, "There's nobody left for their army to draft; all the men are either in the army or dead."

Lester brought up the wider strategic picture, "Sherman is in South Carolina now. If he can make it to Virginia, Sherman and Grant have Lee in the jaws of a vise. There's no other real Confederate army outside of Virginia. If Sherman keeps moving, we can finally go home."

Wilbur, for a change, seemed to have become a more attentive listener, perhaps a result of his habit of listening to the officers in camp. "Nobody wants this war to last one day longer than necessary. The North is sick of war and half of these poor Southern wretches don't even care who wins. Lincoln knows this and so does Grant. He must be concerned that Rebel armies will break up into small guerrilla units and prolong the rebellion for untold months. That's what typically happens with an unsuccessful rebellion. We're not in the days of McClellan and Buell. Grant and Sherman will not stop until the job is done. I think they're keeping a powerful cavalry corps ready to strike a coup de grace on the Confederacy."

"Where?" asked a skeptical Grrr. "There's nobody

left to fight north of the Gulf. We would be more useful trying to keep the peace here."

Hubert, growing more bellicose by the day, roared, "Cavalry is not a peacekeeping outfit! We're ready for offensive action!" Jasper noted how Hubert's courage was highest when up against an outnumbered enemy.

When Wilbur finally offered his take, he began, "You don't walk away from a campfire with coals still hot. This rebellion won't end till all the hotspots are extinguished. And Grant will see to that."

"You mean the Trans-Mississippi? We won't go there!" protested Jasper.

Wilbur nodded, "Of course not. It's a side-show, a scrap heap for discarded generals. There will be die-hards in the Deep South who won't accept defeat no matter what Lee does. They'll rally around anything that's left. The area south of here is still in operation producing war materials. Industry in Selma and Montgomery, Alabama and the part of Georgia that Sherman missed needs to be destroyed."

Hubert looked pleased at the prospect of a destructive raid through the Cotton Belt. "Grrr says there's no opposition north of the Gulf and we're armed to the teeth anyway."

"Except for Forrest's cavalry and he's likely to be under-strength," added Wilbur.

Jasper objected, "*Forrest* and *under-strength* are not words that belong together! He's most dangerous when he's outnumbered!"

Wilbur reassured the others that Forrest's cavalry had lost many of its experienced troopers and some of those remaining were riding on worn-down mounts barely suitable for transportation. Hubert lost track of the conversation after he heard the name *Forrest.* For the rest of the evening, he remained subdued. The others could see that Hubert was looking forward to a mounted rampage through cotton country more keenly than a real battle.

The last campaign

Speculation ended when it was announced that the entirety of Wilson's corps, comprising three divisions, would be saddling up on March 22 for a massive raid through the South's industrial heartland. Croxton's brigade would once again be in Edward McCook's division. The chief target was Selma, which was the Confederacy's largest producer of armaments, gunboats, naval ordnance, and various other products from iron works and foundries. The Selma Armory alone employed ten thousand workers. Nearby coal mines were essential to iron production. Destroying Selma's operations would be a major step in a campaign to exhaust the South's remaining industrial base and transportation system.

Twelve thousand mounted men, along with 1,500 more on foot until mounts could be procured along the way, marched south at a rapid pace, encumbered only by an essential four-gun battery of horse artillery, pontoon trains, and supply wagons. When the corps approached Elyton, site of the later Birmingham, Wilson described it as "a poor, insignificant Southern village, surrounded by old field farms," and the countryside as "poverty-stricken and having an uninviting appearance." After considerable demolition work, Wilson detached Croxton's brigade of 1,500 men to raid Tuscaloosa, while Wilson would lead the main force to Selma and Montgomery.

Both columns ended up fighting skirmishes with portions of Forrest's cavalry, which had remained scattered throughout the region. Once Wilson approached Selma, Forrest had consolidated some of his forces in effort to defend the city. Wilson brought the outnumbered Forrest to battle in the open field and soundly defeated him. With little opposition left, Wilson laid waste to the war industry in Selma, Montgomery, and Columbus, Georgia.

While Wilson was still in Alabama, Croxton was made aware of one of Forrest's divisions under Red Jackson between Elyton and Tuscaloosa. Since it outnumbered his own brigade, he managed to avoid a major battle until Jackson attacked his camp on April 1, where Croxton lost sixty men in killed, wounded, missing. Still, the brigade entered Tuscaloosa with no opposition because Red Jackson's division had to rejoin Forrest, though he arrived too late for the Selma battle. At Tuscaloosa, Croxton destroyed its military assets, along with the university. He was expected to reunite with Wilson but in order to avoid Rebel cavalry, he had to swing north of Wilson's main route. The brigade lost communication with the main force, and encountered swollen rivers and little forage, but the men pressed on. Croxton's brigade arrived in Macon, Georgia on April 29, nine days after Wilson had ended the campaign there.

Macon – the fighting ends

News of Lee's surrender at Appomattox Courthouse

on April 9 had reached Croxton while his brigade was still in the saddle. As the men neared Macon, they met the first of Lee's soldiers on their way home. They were a despondent-looking lot, most in uniforms reduced to rags, some shoeless, all of them looking starved. Their Northern counterparts were provided with rail and river transport, but the Southern rail system was inadequate where it existed at all. As they trudged down the crude roads, men in small groups or traveling alone were often in danger from Unionists seeking revenge and robbery by lawless armed bands growing even more numerous. Wilson's men had been through much of the country that these defeated Rebels were returning to and could only feel pity for what they'd find on arriving.

The Confederate armies in the Carolinas, Gulf Coast, and the Trans-Mississippi were not covered by Lee's surrender, so Wilson's troops were still officially at war. It was not until April 26 that Joe Johnston's surrender to Sherman was signed in Durham, North Carolina. In the meantime, word of President Lincoln's assassination reached Croxton's camp when the brigade was still withdrawing from Alabama. Lester was tending to his horse and talking with Jasper when another soldier from an Iowa regiment came up to them with the news. The man was trying to talk while the emotion choked his voice, "President Lincoln was shot by some deranged Virginian. It happened while he was watching a play at the theater!"

Lester and Jasper stood there trying to come to grips with the information. "This war is finally won and this happens!" Jasper despaired. "What will happen next?"

Lester's reaction, like that of so many of his comrades, was a mix of bewilderment and anger. "Our success was possible only because Uncle Abe wouldn't give up. Nobody else could have won this war."

"Does that mean the short man from East Tennessee is President?" Jasper wished it didn't.

Lester nodded, the reality still sinking in, "The Army can probably keep military control now that Lee and Johnston have surrendered. The Confederacy is dead, its people resigned to defeat. What I worry about is the behavior of men in our camps toward the nearby population. I hope our officers can keep order."

When the pair walked back to camp, they could instantly tell that the news had reached everyone in the regiment. Men were standing around in small knots or gathering at the campfires. There was only one topic, but the assassination provoked a range of reactions. Officers throughout the Union camps were justifiably concerned that the fragile peace just achieved might be endangered by calls for revenge that arose from many camps. To some, the future of the country was as uncertain as it had been in 1861. Among Lester's mess-mates, the talk revolved around who would be in charge of the country. Nobody regarded Johnson as competent.

For a change, Wilbur spoke first, "At this moment, General Grant is the most popular man in the country and that makes him the most powerful. Sherman is not far behind. Grant will have the support of most members of Congress. He commands over half a million soldiers throughout the country, most of us still in position until the last remnants of the rebellion are extinguished."

Hubert added, "Grant will be President in 1868. I wish he could be in office now."

There was no civil authority in Georgia recognized by the U.S. government. General Wilson, as senior officer in Georgia, was responsible for a variety of administrative duties. He organized patrols to hunt down Confederate leaders who might be fleeing from justice through Georgia. The catch was impressive. Jefferson Davis himself was arrested by a Michigan regiment on May 10 outside of Irwinville. He had been camped with a small group of civilians hoping to reach the Trans-Mississippi, which was officially still at war. Arrested with him were his wife, his Postmaster General, and his secretary. As the troopers were moving in, Davis was found with his head covered by a shawl that his wife had draped over him. Soldiers who discovered him reported that Davis had been disguised as a woman. The myth spread throughout the North and remained accepted for some time. Other patrols captured Vice President Stevens, Governor Brown of Georgia, and the infamous Henry Wirz, commandant at Andersonville prison camp. Davis was transported to Fort Monroe, on the Virginia peninsula, where he was imprisoned for two years, then released without charges. Wirz was not so lucky; he was hanged for war crimes as the only Confederate executed after the war.

A period of mourning in Washington was soon followed by a celebration that accompanied the demobilization of the volunteer armies. Most spectacular was the review of the nation's victorious forces dubbed *The Grand Army of the Republic*. It lasted two full days as the armies marched down Pennsylvania Avenue. The men who served in Virginia marched on the first day; those who served under Sherman on the second. Impressive as it was, the review included only a fraction of all U.S. soldiers. Many others would be mustering out in places far from Washington. Union soldiers would be leaving behind a Dixie they had finally exhausted.

The 4th Kentucky remained in Macon so long that the men were growing more and more impatient to go home. Everybody wanted to get on with his life and put the war behind him. Languishing in Macon brought them into closer contact with Southern civilians than they'd been during most of the war. Lester commented one night on the many displaced citizens of Georgia who were depending on the food and other relief doled out by the U.S. Army. "When they see us, they turn hostile and insulting. They sure do hate the idea of Emancipation and refuse to respect the rights of freedmen. I hope they change their attitude while they're still under occupation."

Wilbur told him no amount of occupation would change things, "It doesn't matter what we do because they're going to remain poor. Their whole economy is in ruins and they know they can't return to the old ways. The freedmen will be made scapegoats. That hostility you witnessed isn't something that goes away."

Grrr offered, "Remember when we were in Nashville and Louisville, we saw freedmen moving into the cities for manufacturing jobs? It has to be safer than living on a farm. There's jobs up north, too."

Lester doubted there were enough jobs in Northern cities to employ that many migrants, stating, "I've seen as much prejudice in the North as in slave states."

Wilbur agreed, "Some places are trying to limit migration of new competition. And trying to bring the South into the industrial age won't be easy, the way people down here resist change. It's like they're a people with no national identity. They're not at home in a country they tried to destroy and now the one they fought for is gone, if it ever really existed."

Jasper had another insight, "Maybe they can just pretend they won the war. They can put up statues of generals in the parks, keep flying their flags, and change facts in all the school textbooks."

A reassuring mail call

When the rail line to Macon was finally back in operation, the men cheered their first mail delivery since camp on the Tennessee River. It had been a much-anticipated personal connection with home and the outside world. At that moment they knew the end of the war was being celebrated all across the North, yet here they remained in depressing Georgia and far from home. Lester used to envy his comrades every time mail call went out, but since his furlough, Gretchen had been a faithful correspondent. He had sent her two letters, received one in Kingston and one in Waterloo, and now he was thrilled when her latest letter caught up to him, two months after it was written. He was enthusiastically tearing open the envelope when his name was called again. The second letter was from his mother, Lorna McGill. He was momentarily undecided on which to read first, through he knew he would be reading both of them again and again. Soldiers routinely read every letter from home several times a day.

When mail call ended, Lester withdrew to a secluded corner of the camp and unfolded a three-page letter from Gretchen. He had been hoping for an encouraging message from this lady who had been foremost in his thoughts, but he never expected the flood of exhilaration and anticipation delivered by each sentence. It was almost as if she had their future all planned. He couldn't wait to share his excitement at mess, but he wanted to read his mother's letter first.

Mother Lorna wrote that she was soon leaving Nashville with Major Connor to marry in Indianapolis. They would be settling into his spacious home near the city's center. She went on to say that Major Connor had located Jake through the commander of one of the regiments that had fought at Nashville in December of 1864. Jake had suffered a leg wound on the second day of battle but was recovering with no permanent damage when Lorna and the major visited him in the Army hospital. She wrote that Jake was pleased when she gave him the address in Cincinnati where Lester's mail was being held.

Nobody in camp looked disappointed after mail call. The men talked excitedly about how soon they would be seeing their folks in person. As these last days slipped by, the men spent much of their time talking about how they would return home profoundly changed by the experiences of the past four years. Most wondered whether they could resume home life without a difficult period of adjustment. For the Rebels, it would be much worse. On one of the last nights in Macon, Jasper turned to Lester, "Do you still have kin back in Tennessee?"

Lester, still full of anticipation, told him, "Everybody I care about is safely out of the upper valley. That's all that matters; there's nothing there for me now. But there is in Cincinnati. At least there was two months ago."

"That letter you were so thrilled over was from that lady you met on furlough, wasn't it?" Jasper concluded. "Is she telling you to cross the Ohio River for good?"

"I'd cross more than one river to leave Georgia and show up at Gretchen's door still in one piece," Lester told him.

Wilbur nodded, "It looks like Ohio for me, too. I had planned to return to Lexington and be actively involved in politics. Now I can't imagine what the political climate will be like after the war, but I've decided to forget about politics and make education my only profession. There are plenty of colleges in Ohio that will be looking for faculty and my military record should be looked on with favor by the people in charge. When I was in college, one of my professors was General Garfield. He's in Congress now. Maybe he'll remember me."

"What are the roads like up there?" Jasper baited him with an obvious mud reference.

The others waited, but he calmly said, "Most of the roads are macadamized, so I can ride in a carriage without even thinking about the surface," refusing the bait.

Turning to Grrr, who was looking especially serene, Wilbur asked, "Are you going back to the Louisville waterfront?"

"This war, with all the desolation and misery we pass through when we're not killing each other on the battlefield – it's been so depressing," Grrr sighed. "I want to do some good for a change. I had the chance to talk with Army chaplains when we were in Nashville and Waterloo. They suggested I attend one of the Bible schools near home and find my way from there. I'll start right now by answering only to my given name, *Gordon*."

Hubert was the only one that the war had made more aggressive. "While we were on this glorious raid, I was convinced that my place is in the cavalry. Instead of fighting a war, the country will need experienced regiments to keep the peace on the Plains," he said proudly.

Jasper was quick to point out, "Instead of fightin' Rebels, you'll be fightin' Injuns."

"They won't tangle with U.S. Cavalry," Hubert stated confidently. "By the way, do you have any plans for after the war? Do you even know where you want to live?"

"Oh sure I do," Jasper said with no hesitation. "I knew that when I enlisted at Camp Dick. I'm going back home, to Lewis County. I never was away from there before and wanted to see more of the country. I've sent most of my pay home and it will be waiting for me. The war never reached our neck of the woods. Our hills are a barrier to any unit larger than a company. Folks don't want outsiders telling us what to do. My plan is to stay there and never think about war again."

"Can you make a living up there with no level ground to farm?" Gordon asked him.

"Oh sure you can," Jasper proudly claimed. "Corn grows on the hillside, hogs can root anywhere, and cows have shorter legs on one side so they can stay level on the hillside."

Gordon was ready to point out that the mutation limited the cow to walking in only one direction before he sensed this might be a joke, so he said instead, "Ain't you worried the government will find your still?"

Jasper did his best to look startled and blurted, "The gummint will never find my st...I mean what still?"

It's over!

By the time that the 4th Kentucky Mounted was ready to go home, Wilson had found enough qualified railroad men to repair the track all the way to Tennessee. This enabled the creation of supply points where trains could deliver rations, fodder, and needed equipment for the regiments as they rode north. Days in the saddle were spent retracing the route of Sherman's Atlanta campaign, so the men were not surprised at what they saw, just saddened.

They were leaving behind a land whose citizens had fought the war until they could fight no more. Lester and his comrades wondered whether the South would ever recover from the massive destruction, twenty-five percent of the military-aged men dead, and many others disabled. By now, most of the regiment favored emancipation, but were not optimistic about the plight of nearly 4 million newly-freed people throughout the South. More Amendments could be passed, but the toxic attitudes held by many were only aggravated by the war.

Louisville at the end of the war served as a transportation center for Western troops returning home. Rivers and railroads distributed men throughout the U.S. The five men who had served together throughout the war were at last saying their good-byes, knowing it was unlikely they would be meeting again. Each had a plan for a civilian life that would take him in a new direction, but each was returning home with the satisfaction of duty well-served. Adjustments would be hard after a war that had changed both the soldier and the folks at home. Northern people were ready to move on from the dark days of war, while many in the South never would be. Few soldiers wanted to tell war stories and few at home wanted to hear them. This arrangement was fine with Lester; he wanted to forget all he had witnessed during the past four years.

Lester was hoping to arrange passage to Cincinnati quickly and leave this madhouse. He had mailed a letter to Gretchen after reaching Macon, but it took some time before mail could be sent over a reliable route. In his letter he wrote that she should expect him in July or August, but beyond that only the Army knew. There was a transport going upriver in the morning, so all that remained was to reach Cincinnati without falling off the boat.

Chapter 10
The Fruits of Victory

Long before the end of the Confederacy, a young slave girl was sold to a wealthy family in Memphis. She worked on the staff of the mansion, where she learned the ways of Memphis's cosmopolitan society. She had a brother somewhere, but they had been separated in 1858. Her name was Phoebe and her mind was active. When the Second Confiscation Act was passed in July 1862, contraband camps began to spring up, four in Memphis alone after the city's surrender to the U.S. Navy. When the time seemed right, Phoebe picked up a sack containing her few belongings and confidently strolled to the nearest camp without encountering any interference.

Phoebe had learned to identify many written words when she saw them, but like most arrivals in camp, she was driven to attain full literacy and to gain as much knowledge as she could. A school was among the services provided in the camp, so Phoebe attended regularly. She was able to find some menial employment in the camp and began saving what she could. She had come from comfortable quarters in a mansion to conditions sometimes bordering on squalor, but she now had the freedom to take control of her own life. Simple tasks like saving money, making purchases, and being able to wander outside the camp without supervision were little freedoms she delighted in.

As Phoebe gained knowledge, she also developed a strong sense of self-reliance. She was not satisfied with going from being considered property to someone dependent on the government, charity, or exploitive employers. As bright as she was, she understood that it would take some time to feel really free. The Emancipation Proclamation was just an essential first step toward freedom.

Memphis became a well-fortified city in Union hands. The elaborate works were heavily garrisoned by units that included U.S.C.T. regiments. The city was swelling with freedmen and white refugees, soldiers, Northern businessmen and merchants, and river traffic. Sometimes at night Phoebe lay awake imagining boarding one of the towering riverboats that sat in port building up steam pressure for a cruise upriver to the Ohio. It was later in 1863 that Army personnel visited the camp to recruit volunteers for the U.S.C.T. Several new infantry companies were raised from the Memphis camps. Knots of recruits were waiting to be formed into units and go through the enlistment process. Phoebe was walking past some recruits when she thought she recognized one man by his gait, which gave the appearance of someone trying to reach a destination in as few strides as possible. When she heard him speak to another recruit, she walked up to him and asked, "Alvin? From Scott County?"

"Yes, Miss, and who might you be?" he kindly asked.

"I'm Phoebe, from the Clifton place. My brother is Jake. Do you know where he is?" she blurted.

Alvin told her, "Last I saw him was when him and Miss Hannah took the train out of Knoxville a year ago. The rest of us left the farm for Chattanooga right after the battle there. Me and Sam tried to enlist there, but they weren't forming any more units, so the soldiers sent us to the Corinth camp. We were just there for a few days when the Army closed the camp and sent us all to Memphis. And now we're in the Army!"

"Do you know where Jake went?" Phoebe was sounding anxious.

"All he could talk about was joining the Army. They weren't recruiting men in Nashville for the U.S.C.T. till later in 1863, but I'd be surprised if he didn't stay there waiting for the chance. Most volunteers from that area are in Nashville, serving garrison duty. It's hard to find anyone in the Army," Alvin reported.

"I wish I could be there to look for him. With all the violence between here and Nashville, I can't go anywhere," Phoebe lamented.

"Someday you might find a way there. I don't know if it's possible to find a boat to take you. Maybe you should wait, though. It's still dangerous on the river," Alvin cautioned.

"I know. I'll have to use my time here to save enough for a ticket if they'll sell me one. I'm still not really free till they let me on," Phoebe sighed. She knew she'd have to be patient and did her best to find diversion.

When recruiters came into camp again, Phoebe tried to approach the officers for any information they had on U.S.C.T. soldiers in Nashville. After being ignored or rudely dismissed by several, she found a lieutenant who would listen to her. "When would he have enlisted?" he asked to narrow down possibilities.

"He escaped from Scott County to Nashville in late 1862, but I don't know what he did before recruiting started," she answered.

"That early in the war, Nashville needed a lot of labor to fortify the city. The work was not pleasant and when the first units were formed in August 1863, recruits were kept mostly in Nashville to garrison the city. You'd have to go much higher up than a lieutenant to find him on muster rolls," he apologized.

Often when Phoebe had time off from the work she did in camp, she liked to walk down to the waterfront and watch the various river craft plying the waters of the Mississippi. Many of the workers on the dock were freedmen she came to know. They talked about life on the river, with all the activity afloat and on the banks. They all enjoyed Phoebe's visits, which always brought cheer to the docks.

Phoebe and people she knew in camp had always been closely following the progress of the war. Sherman was pushing toward Atlanta and there wasn't a Rebel soldier left in Tennessee. After Atlanta fell in September of 1864, they cheered the ensuing reelection of President Lincoln. Phoebe's group talked more and more about the coming of peace in Tennessee. Then, when Hood's army was marching toward Nashville, the residents of Memphis knew they were in a secure spot, but a Confederate army meant cavalry raids and roaming desperados without any constraints on their conduct. West Tennessee would have to be purged of Rebels before Phoebe could travel to Nashville safely.

Her strolls to the waterfront were becoming more frequent. She found the constant activity with boats coming in and out, workers, passengers, cargo handlers, and uniformed officials presented a more cheerful scene than the camp. Phoebe met a dock worker named Wally, who had been free since 1862, as one of the first to benefit from the Confiscation Act. He was telling her that he could probably find a way to get her on a boat up the Ohio River. She didn't invest all her hopes in Wally, though, and continued to seek various means.

The guns in Nashville could not be heard in Memphis, but word of the battle arrived when the Federal cannons were still smoking. Thomas had crushed Hood's army and driven the remnants out of Tennessee. Sometime in February 1865, one of Phoebe's visits to the waterfront led to Wally introducing her to Luther, who was a steward on one of the larger craft that ran between Memphis and Cincinnati, and sometimes Pittsburg. Luther had grown up on an Illinois farm, which had suffered financially when navigation on the river was still blocked by Confederate forts and gunboats. When residents in Luther's community celebrated the reopening of river travel once Grant took Vicksburg, Luther's curiosity about life on the river was sparked and he left the farm for the port city of Cairo, Illinois. The Union Army had begun conscripting men in 1863, and Luther could claim an exemption as part of a critical supply system. "Soon I should be able to persuade the captain that I need an extra hand on one of our upriver cruises. Keep watching for the *Lady Monarch* next time we're in port."

"Thank you Luther. Once this war is over, the traveling should be safer," she said.

"I worry more about how Phoebe can travel up the Cumberland once she gets off in Paducah," Wally suggested. "There's still a lot of hostile secesh up there."

Luther was more positive on that aspect. "Paducah has been under our control for three years. All that traffic to Nashville will continue long after the war, so you should easily find a helpful Yankee captain. Remember, you have been free since 1863."

"I may feel free if I left this city. There is so much hostility here. I hope I can find Jake and go somewhere peaceful," Phoebe replied.

She kept track of all announcements of boats docking at and departing from Memphis. River traffic was heavy, but there was no Lady Monarch on the list until nearly May 1865. She managed to find Luther when he came ashore. Keeping in mind that changes were occurring every day during this war, Phoebe braced herself for disappointment. She went right to the point, "Can you find me a place on the Lady Monarch?"

Luther nodded. "I wasn't sure you'd still be in Memphis by now, but I've talked with the first mate, who agreed you could help me in the storeroom and sometimes they may need you in the galley. We'll be departing Memphis in two days. I'll see you Thursday morning at 8:00."

After this encouraging news, Phoebe walked through Memphis for one last look. Peace was coming soon, but you'd never know it from the looks of the city. U.S. soldiers were seen everywhere. The hostility harbored by the citizens toward the U.S. Army and the growing population of freedmen was also fully evident. Phoebe wondered if every southern town was like this. She didn't know whether Nashville would be any better, but the prospect of finding her brother outweighed any apprehensions.

When the Lady Monarch was ready to depart, Luther taught Phoebe the rudiments of her job. She learned how to identify various items in the store-room that often needed to be brought above-deck to replenish supplies as they ran low. The work was tiring, but when the Lady Monarch docked at Paducah, she immediately began seeking a mode of travel up the Cumberland to Nashville. One person told Phoebe that if she took a boat that docked at Clarksville Tennessee, she'd be safer staying on board until it completed the trip. Eventually, she found a small transport carrying a few soldiers to Nashville and the skipper agreed to take her aboard. There was plenty of space, since more soldiers were leaving Nashville than arriving now that the war was over.

The unfamiliarity of the city was daunting at first, but Phoebe found her way to Army headquarters. As usual, most officers ignored her requests for information on a U.S.C.T. soldier with only the name Jake to go on. Several regiments were on garrison duty in Nashville, so she persisted in approaching officers at each camp. One captain she met remembered that Major Connor had been asking about this same soldier and told her how to reach his headquarters. She found the major at his desk and he greeted her cordially, "Private Clifton was wounded on the second day of battle against Hood. He took a minié ball to the leg, but it healed without requiring amputation. Come; I'll take you to his camp." On approach, the major pointed out a tall, fit-looking young man with just a hint of a limp.

Phoebe took it from there. Still some distance away, she shouted, "Jake!" and only one soldier turned toward the voice. He stood there stunned for a second as he recognized his sister.

"Phoebe? How did..." were the only words he could get out before they closed the distance between them and brother and sister were again family. They withdrew to an unoccupied grassy area and sat there for the rest of the day, talking non-stop about the events in their lives that had brought them to this wonderful moment.

The fighting had ended with the surrender of the remaining Confederate armies, but the confusion created by war remained for millions. Jake and Phoebe faced an uncertain future in the wake of this national upheaval. Both had acquired some employable skills, but jobs were scarce where they were. Freedmen usually could not acquire their own land, while share-cropping consigned them to perpetual poverty. Many who had been in the camps chose to remain in the cities where manufacturing jobs were sought. Jake looked at the situation realistically, "We can't stay in Nashville. There's nothing here but a life of struggle. The only real chance we have right now is to go North. There may be work in Cincinnati, but I'm still waiting to find out."

"Cincinnati? Ohio? It has to be far better than here! Who's supposed to let you know?" Phoebe had become excited.

Jake asked, "Do you remember Lester McGill from Scott County?"

"You mean that skinny boy who used to do odd jobs and was scared of everything but horses?" Phoebe certainly remembered.

Chuckling, Jake answered, "Well, he was not too scared three years ago when he joined a Union regiment in Kentucky. We were both in the battle here in Nashville last December but I never saw him then. But I met his mother when her officer friend brought her to see me at the Army hospital. She gave me an address in Cincinnati where a lady was holding Lester's mail. I wrote to him in March, but he hasn't replied. Last I heard, the whole corps under Wilson left on a raid through Alabama and Georgia. They were in Macon when the main Confederate armies surrendered. I don't know when Lester will make it to Cincinnati, but I hope it's soon."

Adjustments

While Jake and Phoebe were pondering their few options, Lester was steaming up the Ohio River, his thoughts alternating between anticipation and apprehension. Gretchen had sent her most recent letter three months ago and much can change in that time, especially in the confusion of civil war. Gretchen was not someone lacking in suitors, so Lester cautioned himself not to take anything for granted.

When he stepped onto dry land, he had no trouble remembering the route to the home of Gretchen's family. He set out at a metered pace down streets lined with houses and shops. In a few minutes, he discovered that after spending the last year of the war on horseback, he could still march as if on campaign as an infantryman. His solo march through Cincinnati was nothing on the scale of the Grand Review in D.C. A song popular at the time promised that, "the men will cheer and the boys will shout; the ladies they will all turn out," but this was not Lester's experience. A few men stared and the only boys around were pretending to be in combat, shouting *bam-bam* from their imagined muskets.

This was not much of a homecoming so far, but as Lester turned onto Gretchen's street, he could see her sitting on the front porch. All doubts that had troubled him vanished when she squealed with delight as soon as she caught sight of her soldier striding toward her. She scampered down the steps to meet him and soon they were inside the Gerlach house. To Lester, this was his first home in four years, yet he couldn't really call it home when he lived under another man's roof. He kept telling himself it would have to do for now but he would not let himself get used to it.

Since last seeing Gretchen, Lester had been in the saddle from the start of the Atlanta campaign to the capture of Jefferson Davis. He had witnessed scenes that still haunted him and declined to relate any of his experiences when asked. Right now, it was a peaceful future that mattered. As he and Gretchen talked, he found a way to express his need for gainful employment. Gretchen assured him her father had a place for him in his plant.

"Oh! I just remembered," she added, "I've been holding a letter that came from Nashville back in March. Let me get it."

She returned with a letter sent by Jake, whose name she remembered from Lester's description of his Scott County days. On reading the letter, Lester was glad that Jake had recovered from his wound and was about to be mustered out in Nashville. It was clear that Jake needed a way to earn a living and that Tennessee was no place to find one. After re-reading and folding the letter, Lester updated Gretchen on Jake's service in the Army, his wounding in battle and his long convalescence in camp.

The Gerlach family had taken a liking to Lester during his furlough and made no attempt to conceal it. Of course in 1865, an unmarried woman of 25 was considered perilously close to becoming an old maid. That evening, there was a sumptuous feast unknown to soldiers below the rank of brigadier general. Afterward, Mr. Gerlach summoned Lester into his study where, instead of a dessert wine, they partook of his private stock of twenty-year-old single-malt scotch. Lester had always been good at judging a man's sincerity from his way of speaking. He had known his share of dishonest men, and Mr. Gerlach was clearly not one of them. It was necessary to trust this man who could greatly influence his life.

The old man began, "Mrs. Gerlach and I left Germany in 1849 with the children after the revolution failed. We came to America with thousands of others. Many of us settled in Cincinnati, Milwaukee, and Saint Louis. Some are even generals in the U.S. Army, like Siegel and Schimmelpfenning. It didn't take long to see that *land of the free* stops at the Ohio River. We started out here living hand-to-mouth, but I managed to open a small machine shop and keep it profitable.

By the time the war began, I was in a position to contract with the War Department for supplying a variety of iron products. It took me years to reach that point, while in the South, arrogant planters are sitting on their verandas accumulating wealth by enslaving others."

"Cincinnati is heavily Republican, but there was a Confederate faction here until Appomattox. They made some political speeches but never caused any real trouble. In Cincinnati I was protected and getting rich off military contracts while you fighting men took all the risks. If you decide to settle in Cincinnati, there will be a job for you. I know you have some experience in farriage, so your skill with tools will be valuable to the company. The shift from wartime production to filling peacetime needs will require skilled workers to help in the changeover. We can still produce boilers and other parts for steamboats and locomotives, but we'll have to make modifications to produce for new uses, such as farm equipment. In a short time, the country will be importing the Bessemer steel-making process from England. It can produce steel in large quantities in a small fraction of the time required now. The only reason for the delay was the war. Soon, steel will replace wrought and cast iron in most everything."

The talk drifted informally to other subjects while Lester still braced himself for the pressure to marry Gretchen. At one point, Gerlach asked Lester if he had to leave any family behind in Tennessee.

"I saw my mother in Nashville last December, but she should be in Indianapolis by now. She's marrying a major in the volunteers whose family owns a retail store there," Lester replied. "I do have a friend in Nashville named Jake, who helped me escape from Scott County into Kentucky. He escaped later and joined the U.S.C.T. in Nashville. He wrote me a letter, care of Gretchen, in March or April from his garrison camp. He's mustering out soon after two years of service in the infantry and being wounded in the Battle of Nashville. The cavalry was on the opposite end of the line of battle, so I never saw him for the rest of the war. I hope I can do something for him now that the war is over."

"Gretchen told me about your experiences in Scott County," Gerlach said as he grew increasingly impressed with this rural lad whose attitudes ran contrary to Confederate tenets. Lester related a little more about people in Eastern Tennessee, but thought it prudent not to mention Hannah.

"Prospects for Jake are not good in Tennessee. If your company has any need he can fill, he's a very capable man," Lester pressed the issue.

"If Jake can make it to Cincinnati, I'll make sure he has something to give him a good start here. The other workers will accept him," promised Mr. Gerlach.

"I'll write to him at once," a grateful Lester responded. "I hope he's still where he can receive mail." Lester was still waiting for the old man to promote his daughter, but he never even alluded to the issue.

The rest of the evening was spent with the family and a couple men from the Ohio regiment he had met during his furlough. At some point, Lester's mind began to drift away from the ongoing conversation. In a bit of déjà vu, the moment had provoked the same feeling he'd experienced his first night with the 4th Kentucky at Mill Springs. Back then, his comrades in the regiment were his new family. With them, he became experienced in the arts of fighting and destruction, but they were of no use to Lester now. He was living in an industrial city already shifting back to the business of peace. He was suddenly brought back to the moment by Gretchen's voice asking, "What would you like in your coffee?"

"No coffee for me tonight. I've had an active day and need to catch up on my sleep," Lester yawned. He was lodged in a comfortable room on the second story of the spacious Gerlach home. The bed seemed soft in all the right places. Comfort like this should have been lulling him into a peaceful sleep, but that was before secession, the war, and the bitterness that still beset much of the land. The guns were now silent and he was far from the theater of war, yet images from the last four years were still keeping him awake every night.

In the morning, Lester penned a hasty letter to Jake and hurried to send it on its way. He noticed how the population of Cincinnati was swelling with refugees, both White and Black, who were seeking employment. Many Northerners were hostile toward competition for jobs or simply toward outsiders in general. Lester was glad to know that Jake had a job waiting for him. This last thought was still on Lester's mind when Gretchen offered to show him the Ernst Gerlach Iron Works plant on the waterfront in eastern Cincinnati. The size of the operation impressed him. Inside the buildings, workers were operating giant machines that produced a variety of iron products.

Since Lester would soon be working here, he asked Gretchen where most of the employees lived. She told him, "Some of them come from families in Cincinnati. Some men come in alone and find a place near work until they learn their way around the city."

Lester took note of the homes and rooming houses near the plant and they seemed clean and habitable enough to give a worker a place to hang his hat.

The evenings that Lester spent with Gretchen proved to be enlightening. As people become better acquainted, characteristics that escaped notice early-on begin to surface. Lester was originally drawn to Gretchen because he had never received this kind of attention from one so bright and charming. He had tried to dismiss any idea that Gretchen was growing desperate at 25. Now he was discovering that Gretchen was not at all concerned with being an old maid in a few years. He gathered this much from bits of their conversations. She was an independent person with no intention of standing in a man's shadow. She had rejected a couple men earlier who mostly wanted deference and children. At some point, Lester began to wonder if he was prepared to put himself in a dependent position. He was staying in her family's house, working for her father, and depending on him for Jake's employment. "I'll keep this to myself for now and maybe I'll figure this out." Lester knew he was inexperienced, and this made him cautious. Meanwhile, they kept enjoying their time together.

Nashville V: No future here

It was still August when mail call brought Jake the welcome reply from Lester. The few lines told him all he needed to know – Lester's wish that he would come to Cincinnati after mustering out. There would be paid work and a place to live safely. Jake showed the letter to a delighted Phoebe and they rejoiced for some time before they turned to practical matters.

"My regiment is mustering out in a few days. The garrison men will have transportation to Louisville at least. This is our chance, Phoebe!" Jake declared. "North of the Ohio!"

"It will be better than here, much better maybe, but life up North won't be easy," Phoebe cautioned. "We both saw cities filling up with people looking for work. Memphis was threatening to turn violent when I was leaving. We'll have to be careful in Cincinnati."

Jake and Phoebe caught the train to Louisville a few days later. The track was by now well-maintained and no longer vulnerable to the likes of Morgan or Forrest. The many ruins and scars on the land were still visible. After a night in crude accommodations in Louisville, brother and sister were on a transport steaming upriver to Cincinnati. The day was sunny, so they enjoyed the fresh air out on the deck. Once they disembarked, they took a few minutes to compose themselves. Jake reassured Phoebe, "It's alright, Sis; I'm in a U.S. Army uniform. We won't have any trouble with folks here."

Phoebe joked, "What if they saw you walking through town with a White woman?"

"In Tennessee, they'd think she owned me," Jake chuckled.

A man carrying some sort of tool kit was walking by them and Phoebe stopped him to ask, "Do you know the way to the Gerlach house?" as Jake was ready to tell him the address.

The man was probably in his sixties and apparently had immigrated recently. He thought for a moment before simplifying their quest with, "It's a long walk to the house, but his business is just five minutes that way," as he gestured east, upriver. "Mr. Gerlach should be there now. He works hard, that man. You're a Union soldier. He likes that."

The pair soon reached the complex of covered areas and buildings behind a sign that read *Ernst Gerlach Iron Works*. This was a working industrial plant, not a plantation, so little was invested in aesthetics. The door with the most in-and-out traffic seemed to be the main entrance, so they ventured on in. Once inside, they saw a large office space, most of it not walled off from the rest of the shop floor. A man nearest the door said indifferently, "If you're looking for work, Mr. Gerlach is gone for the day. Try tomorrow."

Undeterred, Jake asked him, "Do you know a worker named Lester McGill?"

The man suddenly warmed to the visitors. "Oh! Lester! The boss's new hand! You know him from the Army, don't you?" as he introduced himself as Helmut.

"No," Jake smiled, "I knew Lester when I was still a slave in Tennessee. This is my sister who was separated from me for seven years till now."

Helmut was visibly moved by this and told them, "Come. I take you." He led the way to another building where they found Lester at work. Helmut called to him, "Lester! The Army is looking for you!"

Lester had been anticipating this reunion, but that didn't diminish the excitement over seeing Jake for the first time in four years. Jake was understandably travel-weary when he arrived, but beneath this, Lester sensed an energy in him that he'd never noticed before.

"Do you remember my sister Phoebe from the Clifton place?" Jake asked as soon as Lester enthusiastically greeted him.

"I saw you in the garden only two or three times, but I never knew Jake had a sister," Lester smiled at Phoebe. Her eyes sparkled as she returned the smile.

"Whites used to worry about slaves running off to find family. The safest way was not to mention the loss," Jake explained. "I knew Phoebe was sent to Memphis. Once I escaped to Nashville, I tried to find a way to locate her, but nobody could tell me anything about Memphis or its camps. I was hearing that once the war was over, the government would help families reunite, but it was taking too long."

Phoebe added, "The Army couldn't help me much either. When I came to Nashville in May, I wasn't even sure Jake was there at all, but Major Connor led me right to him."

"Major Connor! My new step-dad!" Lester laughed. "Thank God for men like him! Look, my shift will be over in a while. Why don't you wait for me under the shade trees outside the gate? Then I can show you the living quarters I found for you. It's a little tight for two people, but it will be a roof over your head for now."

Work finished for the day, the three walked a short distance and stood in front of a small cottage that looked at least habitable. A few essential furnishings were inside. Lester was almost apologetic for the shabby dwelling when he told them, "You can easily find a better place once you both are working. Mr. Gerlach offered to cover the first week's rent, so it's yours now."

As Jake replied, "This is our first true home!" it was plain to Lester that Jake was genuinely delighted with the right to live where he chose. "And a job that pays wages – I hope."

"Gerlach says you do," Lester assured him. "I don't know how enjoyable you'll find the work. Most industrial jobs are not glamorous, including mine. But the company pays well and conditions are decent."

"Jake!" Phoebe jumped in. "Remember the newspaper story!"

"It's right here," as Jake brought out a carefully-preserved clipping from the Knoxville Whig, whose editor was William Brownlow, a well-known Unionist throughout the war. The column was dated April 3, 1865:

Scott County Still at War!

The body of a slain man was discovered in a wooded area outside of Huntsville, seat of Scott County. Local citizens have identified the victim as Slade Clifton, a former resident who had left the area in late 1862.

He had reportedly returned last week and confronted squatters who occupied the abandoned farm. Threats were made, but there were no witnesses to the killing. Slade Clifton was a vocal secessionist before Burnside's occupation of Knoxville. His wife, Ella Monroe Clifton, had succumbed to illness during the removal of residents from Atlanta following occupation by Sherman. A son, Willard, served in the Confederate army until mortally wounded at Perryville in 1862. A sole surviving relative, daughter Hannah Clifton, was last seen leaving Nashville.

Lester commented without showing emotion, "Hannah was a fine person with the courage to reject the teachings she grew up with. Mother said Hannah was planning to attend school in Ohio, much further north." As Lester talked, he realized that the home he had left in Scott County no longer existed. The tranquil simplicity of life was shattered and the region would not know peace for some time to come. "My friends are right here with me and Cincinnati is our new home," he said with no real regret.

As Lester was leaving for the Gerlach house, Jake asked him when he'd be expected at work. "Helmut will expect you day-after-tomorrow at 8 A.M. You'll hear the chimes on the City Hall clock. It doesn't give you much time to settle in, but I knew you'd want to start on the payroll right away. If you and Phoebe need any help, let me know," adding, "See you at work."

Home on the Ohio

Lester walked slowly as he made his way back to Gretchen's house in order to give himself time to reflect on events of the past few days. He was grateful in knowing that everyone he cared about was safe and secure. His only source of anxiety was the uncomfortable dependence on a rich man's daughter, but he thought it best not to make any life-changing decisions just yet. For now, he had to be content with shoring up his scarce resources. The farrier trade was still in demand, but tools and workspace for any trade cost money that he didn't have. He had been well-acquainted with thrift all his life, so he could add some of his pay to what he had saved during his three years in the Army. He just needed time to learn about life in the city.

On reaching the Gerlach home, Lester found the others already sitting down to dinner. He took his usual seat at the table and made it a point to study the table etiquette the others were practicing. "This is one of the many things Gretchen would have me learn to be acceptable in Cincinnati society," Lester thought in one of his more cynical moments. He remained quiet but cheerful the rest of the evening.

Over the next few days, Lester was learning his job and becoming more familiar with his surroundings. His walks around town took him past rooms and cottages available to rent. He saw a tiny bungalow that was about the size of his old Scott County cottage that had a small shed in back. He located the man in charge of the property and was satisfied with the amount of rent. A wood stove, a table with two chairs and a bench, a sink and drying board, and a cabinet were among the furnishings in one room. Lighting was provided by two oil lamps, which could be supplemented with candles from the store. The smaller room was for sleeping, but Lester would have to find a comfortable cot.

The next evening, Lester announced to Gretchen,

"I've found a little place with rent I can afford that's closer to work. After four years with no place to call home, it's important...."

"I understand!" Gretchen interrupted. "It's only natural for a man to regain control over his life after everything you did was dictated by the war. I admire your spirit of self-reliance. We're two independent people with a lot to learn about each other. You've stayed remarkably calm in adjusting to peacetime pursuits. It takes time."

Once he retired for the night, Lester had to sift through the last conversation with Gretchen. He felt some relief in knowing he was not expected to act in haste in matters that involved his future. He still had to question Gretchen's observation that he had made a smooth adjustment to civilian life in Cincinnati. "Why does the war still keep me awake at night? I suppose that too will take time. After all, I have a new life here and a promising future, maybe with Gretchen."

The next day, Lester moved his few belongings to his bungalow as soon as the work-day was over. Still early in the evening, he lit his pipe and sat on the front door stoop to collect his thoughts. As he watched the people who were passing by on the sidewalk, he tried to imagine whether any of them had been personally affected by the war. They were probably headed home from their jobs or maybe from the many shops that were just now closing for the day.

"Now I'm one of a multitude who make this city their home, after a war that has left untold thousands with no home at all," he briefly mused before he began to focus on his own future.

His life had been governed by a chain of unpredictable, usually random, events that began in Scott County four years ago. Now in Cincinnati, he could feel once again in command of his own future. He was expecting Jake and Phoebe to come by at 7:30 to celebrate his new home.

"Ironic," Lester reminded himself, "that the man who helped me escape Tennessee is now my neighbor in Ohio!"

Lester had been taking delight in the little amenities that civilians usually take for granted. An intact roof after camping in all kinds of weather was in itself satisfying. He was adding to the list of items that would be useful in his new home when Jake and Phoebe arrived. All three were already in high spirits as they sat at the table where snacks from the nearby saloon and a quart-sized bottle were sitting. Lester could not afford 20-year-old scotch, but nobody complained about the Kentucky sour-mash whiskey. The festive trio sat in Lester's new home for the rest of the evening, never running out of things to talk and joke about. Lester had known Phoebe only from a couple brief interactions, so tonight was his first chance to experience her quick wit and engaging personality, rare for someone that young. Jake had already learned that only a little encouragement was needed for Phoebe to bring laughter to those around her. She announced some of her own good news, "Yesterday I found a job at the Dillon Hotel, serving rich old ladies in the tea room. They put me in a little uniform and now I get paid for what I did in Memphis."

Jake joked, "That's what won her the job; she

knew the ways of high society! Show us what you learned," as Lester began pouring the whiskey.

Phoebe began by chiding Lester for serving whiskey in non-matching metal cups, giggling as she went. Now emboldened by her first tiny dram of 80-proof, she went on, "Why I do declare, Aunt Samantha! That Beauregard lady who supervised the table settings for the *Charity Banquet and Grand Ball* brought the wrong color doilies for under the fingerbowls! And then her husband used his dessert fork for the biscuits! Ask the Tyler's; they saw it. Everybody did! Now that's tacky, just tacky!"

Lester nearly convulsed with laughter, remarking, "If I plan to be in high society, I need to take etiquette lessons from you!"

Jake said, "She's been doing this ever since we left Nashville! We were both so thrilled to make it out of there."

The rest of the evening went on like this, as they mixed hilarity with a little serious talk about the future in Cincinnati. Lester told Jake what Mr. Gerlach had said about the many adaptations to new products and materials that lay ahead, "There's no bright future in blacksmithing and farriage. I think working for Gerlach is a good way to learn new skills that will pay off later. Then maybe we can open our own shop."

Phoebe cautioned Lester, "Then you'd better stay on the right side of Miss Gretchen in the meantime!"

"Why?" he smiled, "You're teaching me all the proper manners. I already know about fingerbowls and doilies."

Phoebe kept on, "Next week we'll work on keeping elbows off the table."

Jake looked at her and said, "Go easy, Sis! Lester and I are still getting used to eating indoors! That's a privilege the Army doesn't give you."

"And only officers got whiskey!" Lester gave a comic salute.

The festive evening was approaching 11:00 when Jake told his little sister that they should let Lester get some sleep. "I'm glad you live close-by so we can visit like this more often," Lester told his friends as they were at the door. "We can finally feel at home in a country at peace." After a cheerful *good night, see you at work*, the pair headed home.

It took a little time for Lester to turn in. He went back to his place at the table and reflected on the evening just enjoyed with Jake and Phoebe. The warmth he still felt was not the kind that comes from a bottle; anyway, the one in front of him was still over half-full. He wished he could feel like this all the time. He hoped to start out tomorrow well-rested, so he lit a candle and walked into the tiny room where he slept on a makeshift bed.

After snuffing out the candle, Lester stretched out in the comfort of his snug but quiet home. Tonight he wasn't thinking so much about Gretchen or what lay ahead in his new life. Instead, his mind took him back to 1862 when he first enlisted in the 4th Kentucky. Like many thousands who wore the blue, he had responded to President Lincoln's call to *preserve the Union.* Through much of the war, Lester could see only the destruction and misery that resulted from putting down the rebellion. But then, with the outcome still much in doubt, Mr. Lincoln had given the war new meaning when he spoke of *a new birth of freedom* that would accompany Union victory in the war. The jubilant evening Lester shared with his two closest friends was a celebration not only of peace, but also freedom for Jake and Phoebe and millions more for all time. The profound moment Lester had experienced tonight was still occupying his thoughts as he drifted slowly into his first untroubled sleep since mustering out. For tonight at least, there were no guns of war to keep him awake.

About the Author

Scott Allen Freeman, retired professor, has been a Civil War enthusiast since 1980, serving as a re-enactor, frequent contributor to Civil War newsletters, and speaker/presenter on Civil War topics to various local groups. Two Freeman ancestors fought in the 83rd Pennsylvania Infantry, organized in 1861 by Colonel John McLane, later promoted to Brigadier General. The author is an alumnus of *General McLane High* in Edinboro, PA.